"Whenever you see a board up with 'Trespassers will be prosecuted,' trespass at once." - Virginia Woolf

Printed by Orbital Print
T: 01233 211202

Josiane Van Melle

Trespassers

Cover picture: Marieke Deraed
Cover design: Alicia Gram

ISBN	EAN
978-2-9602037-0-7	9782960203707

www.josianevanmelle.com

1

I think we will be happy here. These were the words to her sons.

First Oak knew it would not take long for the young woman to decide on the purchase of the ruins and the five-hundred acres of fertile land. Nothing to compare with the seven-hundred-acre deer park when Saxingherste was a hunting palace, seventy and three-hundred growth rings ago. The ladies would ascend the lookout tower, dressed like cockatoos, and watch the hunt while the men pursued the terrified deer.

Dressed in trousers and high boots, the young woman now climbs the tower, and at the top, elbows resting on the parapet, she discovers how the black mirror of the moat reflects the flight of the starlings, launched from the high hop poles, further to the west. She can see hares and larks skimming the sweet vernal grass. The nightingale can be heard from two miles away. And in the distance, among the never-ending greens blending into the lachrymose greys of the sky, the shimmering shale of the lake.

Vita, Vita, this is it, the young woman cries, overjoyed. Her gypsy skin feels the weathercock breath of the one and hundred winds.

Inside the tower, her face stretched close to the cold lattice window, Vita sends small puffs of breath. Her index finger draws a rough geometry on the ephemeral clouds. Her husband observes her from the corner of his eye. She need not turn her head as she states the obvious:
- We must restore the walls, Hadji. They will make ideal partitions between the gardens. Wallflowers, toadflax, rosemary will nibble the bricks in easy settlement…
- …The plural form, interrupts Harold. Will we reproduce Lutyens' gardens of Long Barn?

- You will sketch the plans without Sir Edwin. Gardens that will have their own personality and distinct shape. Their own colours too, without too much formality. I will start with a Violet garden.

Behind her back, Harold clears his throat:

- That Violet, you will never get her out of your mind, will you, Viti?

He intended a light tone of voice, but Vita hears the sharp point of his animosity.

- I talk about asters, dahlias, heleniums, verbena… and the rosa moyesii, Hadji. And you talk about Violet from whom I haven't heard for so long! Come to think of it, I have nothing against the Viola odorata because of how it spreads wherever it is happy, so why not let it roam and range as it listeth? When I say violet, Hadji, you must think blue, mauve, purple!

Vita emphasises in a single breath:

- Blue as the Mediterranean on a calm day; blue as the smoke rising in autumn bonfires in our woods; blue seen through the young green of chestnut or beech; blue as the star-cabochon sapphire given to a bride on her wedding-day.

She catches her breath and adds:

- And more important yet, Hadji, hyacinth-scented beyond all these, just a bluebell wood, the expression of the greatest simplicity.

Vita's lips let out a deep sigh. Harold can't make out whether it dresses up as impatience towards him or regrets for the woman Trefusis, source of much sorrow. With a shake of her body, aware of her husband's pain, Vita moves away from the window and comes to sit next to him on one of the camp beds unfolded in a corner. She has spent several nights in the tower on her own while Harold and their sons stayed at Long Barn. Harold prefers his comfort to camping. And the duration of the renovation of Sissinghurst is an unknown factor in his life.

First Oak knows how Saxingherste revealed itself to the tall lady as she approached down the winding lane: like a woman unveils her flesh in slow undress. First, the surrounding woodland and the farm: a smock of unbleached linen. Then, through the porch slightly ajar, the transparency of a chemise, the gardens soon to be revealed. Vita can guess at them; titillated, she wants to reach further than the fuzzy lawn, towards each one of the intimate gardens; a wall of red bricks around some, a belt of secular yews circling others, and the secret coils of the moat. First Oak suspects the gardens will soon become an invite to flirtations, calculated equivocations, telltales of transgressions.

Vita and Harold have climbed down the tower and are walking along a track by the moat. A haycart sits under a large oak tree and further up stand the oast, the barn and the piggery. Vita grabs Harold's hand:
- Imagine, Hadji, a succession of gardens, like rooms which would stretch ad nauseam. A bit like Knole, you see?
Sadness casts a dark tinge to her voice. Harold knows all about his wife's passion for the lordly house of her childhood. A passion that probably exceeds the one she had for Violet Trefusis. Maybe even the love she has for him. Harold closes his eyes, conjures the image of Knole: a calendar house with allegedly as many rooms as there are days in a year, as many staircases as there are weeks, twelve entrance doors, seven inner courtyards, grey walls and a brown-red roof. Not to mention the numerous chimneys that seem inspired with a life of their own. Imagine eighty-five hearths smoking in unison… more like a college of Benedictine monks farting in chorus. The enumeration is enough to make Harold nauseous. Let alone walking through all four acres of rooms, which he had never done when they lived there in the first years of their marriage. Harold opens his eyes:
- Evidently, you will do as you wish, Viti, won't you?

3

Silently, they enter the inner courtyard through the Priest House garden. Vita leans against the wall, her eyes drawn to the tower:

- Can you see, Hadji, how the tower stands in the very heart of Kent? Here is a marriage of culture and nature like nowhere else.

First Oak assumes that it is the tower which prompted Vita to acquire Saxingherste. She saw herself as the compelling centre, within the remains, vestige of the magnificence of the past, promise of impending conquests.

Vita is that tower. It will be her writing haven, her lover's room. She will assume the rightful place that she should have been allotted and was deprived of. She will be seen.

First Oak can see that she already loves that radial point of many past periods, and can foresee future projects; unleash her imaginative schemes. She knows the tower is the much-needed umbilicus which will fasten her heart. She knows all that as her long hand caresses the red brick where arborescent lichens spread in trusting abandon. A brush, a stroke of Vita's hips against the wall; arousal nearing.

2.

The gardeners have lead the assault on the meadows, probed the walls; the hollows resonated in outrage. First Oak is satisfied that they denuded the long wall that was concealed by the rows of filberts; elegant, Elizabethan, smothered by three hundred years of debris, brambles and thorns. First Oak can still feel the vibration inside his vital fluid that the pickaxes caused against the red bricks; his leaves yet shiver from the shouts of surprise of the deflowering gardeners and that of beautiful Vita.
First Oak was cross at Harold's reaction when he discovered the hazel understorey for which himself has nothing but contempt. Those small trees claim their ancestrality to have stemmed in the Mesozoic era! As headstrong as their husks, they can't decide on the number of their stems. It was them, not First Oak, that prompted Harold's decision. He took his wife's hand and together they slipped under the thick shield of the branches; a Sleeping Beauty's shrubbery that Vita wanted to awaken. It will not be the embrace of a prince, but her own which will bring back life to the castle, exuding once again its magic.
Harold laughed, tilted his head to avoid the bite of a branch; he took a tender yellow catkin between two fingers; in dreamy abandon his caress lingered; he hoped for the gonad of its fruits.

- Heaps of wall-space for climbing things, Hadji, and we will cram, cram, cram every chink and cranny.
They are assessing the progress of the hired hands and farmers who are doing the heavy-duty work, as Vita calls it. The inevitable destruction of two crumbling cottages and a lean-to in the Top Courtyard; a ramshackle greenhouse taken down from the right-hand Tower Lawn wall; getting rid of the tangle of nettles, bindweed and ground elder covering junk heaps, and more bric-à-

brac than you can find on the Old Spitalfield Market in London. However, she instructed them to save any odd lump of stone as well as sinks and fireplaces. The sinks will be trough gardens and she has many ideas for the stones.

Once the walls had been uncovered, Vita could intuit her vision of the gardens. Harold is also plotting and planning, and as he reveals his overall scheme, Vita is rather annoyed by his conservatism; he can be such a bore. Harold wants an austere design, while Vita needs excessive passionate profusion. There is a tinge of violence in her voice as she says:

- Masses of shrubs, big groups of flowers. The more the flowers are tight, Hadji, the more they will assert themselves in their beauty. Like women who know they are beautiful, will want to be different from one another.

Vita shrugs, darts her dark eyes at Harold – "profound as pools from which the morning mist had lifted", as Violet Trefusis saw them. Vita stares at Harold's pipe, strong and potbellied like him:

- Cram like you would your pipe, if you prefer. A first layer loosely packed, followed by a good stuffing of the tobacco will allow for a better draw, isn't that so, Hadji?

Harold sighs. Even though he privately smiles at Vita's intelligence, the trouble she goes through to make him listen to reason, he does not have the same vision of a garden. He knows how formality is a necessity. Elegance is the key word for him, lines of demarcation between plural gardens. He thinks that the romantic temperament is, as usual, obstructing the classic. He takes two long drags of his pipe before he declares:

- How can you manage military units, that consist of battalions, regiments, squadrons, and ensure a perfect harmony of the forces in presence?
- This is not a battle ground, Hadji, says Vita, offended.

Battle ground indeed. Vita has not been witness to the violent past of Saxingherste. But he, First Oak, has been aware, having thrived alongside the moat for more than five-hundred growth rings, of everything that happened at Saxingherste and way beyond, extending to an area in miles as broad as his growth rings put side by side. With Vita's arrival, First Oak had visions of major upheavals at Saxingherste. He had felt within the crevices of his bark an improbable tickling, as if his trunk had to stretch out even further to become the stoic witness of imminent changes. First Oak has a better view over the tower and lower ramshackle buildings of what passes for the castle, if one is magnanimous. He will observe, in sometimes discomforting glimmers, the changes in which his premonitions manifested themselves.

Back in the tower which has been restored to make Vita's writing room on the first floor, Vita throws a reproving glance at Harold, fiddles with her pearl necklace as if it were prayer beads for divine intercession:
- If at least you would talk about phalanxes, hand-to-hand combat... The force of the gardens, Hadji, will come from the massive lumps of flowering shrubs.
She continues, a dreamy look on her face:
- A propos, Hadji, the Bacchante, shall we place her at the very end of the Lime Walk?
Harold draws on his pipe. The bowl is getting too warm for his peaceful enjoyment:
- Why not? But, remember, the Bacchantes were at the service of Dionysus.
- What are you hinting at?
- I wish you would consider my suggestions, for one...
- ... And I wish you would consider mine. You draw the skeleton; I add the flesh, isn't that so, Hadji?

First Oak collects his thoughts under the dense canopy gorged with the first spring showers, under which all life flickers and jumps. The sharply frilled leaves of the foliage quiver, the knots tighten around the dormant bud. While First Oak has mixed feelings about the impending changes, he wonders how it would have been in the days First Oak was told about, when the Celts left their imprint around Saxingherste. He boasts about their deep veneration for his specimens, as they recognized the density and durability of their wood. Druids, it is said, attributed healing power to the mistletoe dotted oaks. Circumventing clusters of oak, beech and chestnut trees, the Romans drove a major road that links Three Chimneys and Cranbrook, through Milkehouse which was renamed Sissinghurst. The Northern invaders violated the Great Island's shores to put their hands on the precious wood.

Harold has his sly smile which Vita knows is a defence against his excessive sensitivity. She doesn't know what exasperates her most: his heart-shaped face and protective shell bristled like a nettle, or the hyper sensitivity of the Mimosa pudica which, when tickled, quickly folds up its leaves, collapses its stem and straightens up when you have turned your back. Harold's sulking, like the Mimosa's reflex, is never long-lasting. Vita remembers how their sons laughed at the temporary collapse of the flower when Harold encouraged them to touch it; they would do it again and again. Vita saw it as a harmless outlet for the sadistic streak in children.

Forest and warren, cropped by herds of deer,
And droves of swine that stirred the oak-trees' mast.

First Oak can still hear the satisfied grunts of hordes of hogs and boars which were fattened in the fertile pastureland, and that feasted on the prepuce-covered acorns. His gaze follows the long alleyway which leads to Saxingherste, a convoluted ribbon at the mercy of ditches, sprinkled with mimulus and purple irises, rooted in the wetland.

Harold lets off a grunt. Vita got all worked up about the colour scheme he chose for the cottage garden.

- You object to my ideas… a difficult range of colours, I admit, the deep reds and scarlets you steer clear of. However, in Mexico…
- … mixed with orange! Really, Hadji….
- … A brave and sophisticated palette, Viti, a sunset range of colour. I saw it in Mexico…
- A sort of western sky after a stormy day, interrupts Vita. Why not add Tropaeolum Speciosum or Gloriosa superba while you are at it?
- You only like flowers which are brown or green and you see everything in theatrics, Viti. I claim simplicity.

First Oak knows all about simplicity. He was born along the three-armed moat of the Saxingherste manor laced with watercress, aquatic lilies and horsetail; where the White Admiral flitted, revealing the powdery orange cream of its underwing. Before that, there was the narrow sinew of a river threading through the heavy clay soil, creasing watercourses into the land, swallowing First Oak's seeds. The Weald was impassable woodland, Andredswald as it was named by the Saxons; its clustered trees formed a black shiny marquee. This image triggers another, less comforting for First Oak. He cannot help whisper: There soon will be an access road instead of the undulating ribbon.

His congeners alongside him on the bank of the moat rustle, creak in sceptical boisterousness. First Oak perceives the thoughts that arise in them: nobody can get through; the access is complicated, even impassable, except in the hard, dry months of high summer and early autumn. Only First Oak knows about the stinking black lava flow which will be spewed to allow for motor cars to penetrate Saxingherste. There will be no clay mud in which foxes, deer and badgers leave their imprint in double bar notes, H-natural, as on a musical stave. First Oak cannot help warning: It will be the death of the mud song. The death of the sounds of rurality, replaced by the flat monotone noise of tyres on tarmac.

A suction sound followed by a gurgling of saliva in the pipe. Vita resents that noise. She cannot help the exasperation in her voice:
- I would go for simplicity any time, certainly no ostentation, but I want to cover every inch of each bed to prevent undesirable weeds and...
- ... at least we agree on simplicity.

The death of the mud song. First Oak's words come as a blow. His neighbouring oaks wiggle the tip of their roots to make certain of the reassuring presence of the clay loam. A velvety softness which makes healing poultices of serpentine for their articular aches. Their bark perspires at the threat. After a delayed reaction time for some to recover from their indignation or gnarling, others to regain their solicitude, all revert to their distractions. Each, in contemplation or observation, await First Oak's premonition to be verified.

- I insist on placing my soldiers, says Harold. Sentinel plants, vertical lines, topiary, Irish Yews...
- Your phalluses in other words...
Harold does not object to this last fléchette from Vita. He lets his pipe cool down on the ashtray, removes another one from his herringbone tweed jacket pocket, packs it carefully, glancing at Vita who has already lost interest in him. Applying truce is

10

essential when nearing the risky topic of their respective sexual inclinations.

- I quite like the idea of sentinels, Vita says. It would give me the impression of being protected against the French invaders and their horribly neat gardens.

Vita is satisfied with the compromise she went for with Harold. She has adopted a mantra which she gladly repeats:

- I know that we will be happy here, all four of us.

3.

Vita is weary of French gardens. Is she aware of how the French soldiers damaged the castle during the seven-year war, when Saxingherste had been converted to a prison, many growth rings ago? First Oak had been shocked by the state of the castle after the French prisoners had been released. It was to be expected from more than three-thousand men crammed in the same space, stowed up in dormitories and cells, like a colony of termites: sweat, piss, bashings, scratchings and chippings off by rugged fingers. From men in need of prowess, who lacked collective identity; toned down uniform and buried vainglory. The Glory of Saxingherste Castle forever lost. Even the beams had been used for heating in winter days when a biting frost made First Oak curl up his roots. The men, common seamen used to the slap and sting from the one and hundred winds carried on the crest of waves, had a single wish: to get out in the courtyard for some fresh air, find relief in stupid games that would make their testosterone sap flow more vigorously; some through innovative activities. A few of them fared better than others if they knew how to speak the language of the Great Isle.

One man stood out. Middle-aged, skinny, a long pear-shaped face, nose saluting chin, chiselled lips, tip of a tongue sticking out. A most incongruous face in unequal proportion of clay and rainbow. First Oak is familiar with the mixing of nature's ingredients, where the artist has a butcher's face and the butcher a poet's.

Most of all, First Oak had been struck by the hands of the man: long and thin, fingers like a hazel switch. He folded the supple twigs against his palm to keep them warm and tenderized. Those kindling fingers had given life to many different creations, sculpted from mutton bones. First Oak had been witness to their patient conception and later, he had seen them placed on the well's stone edge: a set of dominoes, a toiletry case, two dogs, all varnished. There was also a vessel, all sails set and flying, a primitive draw, no doubt, but heartfelt. First Oak had known the nostalgia that permeated the man for the Royal Louis. It had been built at the naval arsenal of Brest where, as a young man, he had participated in its building; where he had met with Blaise Ollivier, the reputed engineer who had conceived its plans. The man with the pear-shaped face had helped place the beams supporting the guys on the ship which had been built all the way to the third bridge, before a fire destroyed it completely on dry dock, in no more than six hours on Christmas Day of the year 1742.

The hazel has the property to raise its branches to draw water towards its trunk. First Oak saw the man raise his hands, fingers shell-shaped against his eyes from which water cascaded on his misshapen clay face.

Vita can only see poetry in the land she explores with Martin, her faithful Alsatian, as she now reaches the Hammer Brook. Her decided stride hardly pierces the morning silence. A slight drizzle moistens her face. She wears a Mexican straw hat and her fine earrings shine like golden harvest-moons. Her cheeks are a healthy pink. Her assiduous writing tricks her away from sleep more and more, and the shadows around her dark hooded eyes seem like a trace of Kohl. Her perfectly outlined lips are naturally red.

The Hammer flows leaded grey waters, carrying black silt, ruffling brackens, horse-tail tassels. Trouts draw lemniscates in sunlit pools; acorns dare a plunge with friendly percussion beats. There, where it makes a right bend, past the hops scales, the horizon suddenly opens, Frogmead meadows glisten towards Bettenham Manor. Vita's laced leather boots stumble on the warp and weft of roots. Amber and ginger leaves create the perfect alchemy which in Vita's eyes grants simple beauty, rich smells and celebrates the true return of a season she adores.

It was in the autumn 1760 that another Frenchman, First Oak mainly saw from behind, had distinguished himself. Arms akimbo, ramrod back, curly hair fringing the collar of his grey smock, he would face the pointed towers and map the castle layout on a square sheet of paper with black ink and onion skin dye. First Oak, who sees everything in precise perspective, had laughed at the imperfect geometry of the buildings. The painting was naïve, the figures drawn out of proportion. However, First Oak had been touched as he had recognized himself in the drawing. He had been intrigued by the details of the gate, the middle arch and two subsidiary arches left and right, and the arrogance of the chimneys crouched like pointers. The painter did not miss the small doorway, nor the pair of oak doors. First Oak had heard the sharp hurtful falling of bill and axe on tender wood; the agony of the trees felled in Charts Hill Wood, and others from Bull Wood. Surely, he had thought, he would one day share the same destiny. A shiver runs through his cambium.

But if he took an axe to fell the oak,

Even several oaks, as many as might be,

Then must he pay for three, not more than three,

For axe is an informer, not a thief,

And at the felling loud in protest spoke.

Vita favours no season more than the other, feeling akin to this one for its melancholies in rusty tints; another for its liberated exuberance; a third for the fake sleep and sharp silvery geometrical lines; ultimately, the one gorged with vital fluids which gives birth to so many prodigies. Hasn't she given birth herself to two boys who surprise her with their individuality, as if they should have been of Sackville ground and Nicolson clay? And they are none of that, only two solid segments grown out of estranged soil.

Her eldest gives her trouble. She goes such a seesaw over Benedict, depending on what mood he arrives home with. She can't feel at ease with him and their relationship seems like a motor-car with a clutch that won't get into gear: it grinds and nothing happens, the car won't start off. His aloofness, at times effete nature, does not help to know him better. He can so easily look bored that Vita is tempted to welcome him with secateurs and invite him to work in the garden. And yet, he is so like her. Sedentary by nature, a bookworm rather than a socialite, he has her scholarly turn of mind. He can be kind and yet tactless, taciturn and garrulous. Nigel is easier to deal with. Was she ever more present to her youngest son than she was to her eldest, four years older? Harold sees Nigel as perfect, not an intellectual, but they shall have enough to spare on that in Ben. Vita agrees with Harold's satisfaction with the boys. He had said in a letter that "they will, respectively, satisfy all that we could wish for: Benedict our highbrowness, Nigel our human needs". How right he is.

First Oak's premonition of impending changes at Saxingherste has been confirmed, but he feels rather reassured by the arrival of the couple and their two sons. By Vita's words that said sentinels were important. Nobody but First Oak could fill the void better. And the moat needs the shade he provides for the love dance of emerald blue Demoiselle, riffle beetles, shadflies, which slide on the soft water or fly into the swarm; so that herons too will find protective shade for fishing or sharpening their yellow-billed blade against twisted zephyrs.

The one and hundred winds whistle transformation.

Vita needs reassuring signs, promises of a future. She sees them in everything. Left, along a path, over several yards are neatly stacked rows of cut logs. They tell her of a disrupted life cycle. Trees ripped off their roots to comply with the necessities of a tyrannical society. Vita is one of those trees, uprooted from her beloved Knole, chased out of her paradise like an unwanted insect. Exile lies within, making her heart a desert inhabited by fennecs and snakes. Her stomach knots. Will Sissinghurst succeed in bringing her to the stage of nymph?

She hears the metallic call of pheasants in the rye fields towards Bettenham. Martin in pursuit. Vita's boots sound an alarm that makes a covey of partridge scuttle away. That many signs of abundance and life in a season without pretence, where neither day, nor night claims any urgency. Not that of getting up early, not that of going to bed late. It seems to Vita that even death is a possible evasion. It would come to her as swiftly as the day limply downs, a sfumato effect. Vita likes the uncertainty of contours which allows the imagination to stroll freely. Indecision is not a word for her: it is or it is not. Even though, in the following instant it no longer is, and she can laugh at her own contradictions.

Vita whistles for Martin who turns up like a shot from under the brushes, nestles his wet muzzle in Vita's hand, begging a caress. A few rhymes slip out which she will later enter in her book, a moral relief, unburdening of thoughts. She will need a great calm. A calm that would allow the imperviousness of certain words, the predicament of others, death by crossing out, punctuation like fly speck.

Mistrust the seeming truce, that in the pyre

Of distant woods, and in the gardens' fire,

In pheasants running bronze on furrowed mould,

Burnishes autumn with a coat of gold.

4.

What a shame to have planted the row of Taxus! First Oak knows all about their poisonous inclination; their evergreen presumptuousness despite their dread of water. He has heard rumours about the Yew trees in the ancient cemetery of Ulcombe; some say they would be over three-thousand years of age. It is not surprising at the rate they grow, the like of common reed.

To First Oak, it seems that a fortified wall will soon be raised that will obstruct the horizon. That the gardens, if one is not careful, will soon turn into a labyrinth and that the only escape would be through the airs like Daedalus himself with his son Icarus. There is no way around for First Oak: give him back the uniformed view over meadows; pastures where thirty breeding cows with their Cassiopeia eyes grazed; the scales along which hops grow faster than bindweed. Give him back the primordial activity of forty labourers on the farm. The castle disintegrated in the time of Horace Mann, lost its size and lustre and remained dilapidated for close to a hundred growth rings. First Oak had rejoiced about the arrival in the mid eighteen-hundred measured on human growth scale, of the new tenant, George Neve. The farmer and amateur antiquarian had converted part of the castle into a stable block. He had also built a new farmhouse, dignified and imposing, and the rescued buildings of the castle were lodgings for penniless families. With the cow herds, corn fields, orchards, the farm lavishly dispensed its products, and the Cranbrook villagers talked about the cash cow they unscrupulously milked dry. In addition, the farm provided respectable work for the men that George and his brother had helped out of destitution. They both had seen the profit they could make from cultivating and kilning hops; they built kilns adorned by bonnet-shaped cowls, and a milk house against the setting sun. First Oak remembers Richard in particular. A man with lamb's eyes, the glossy brown of an acorn. A woman's sensitivity as he assisted with the calving, applying cataplasms of clay and lanceolata broth on their wounds. He was in charge of the vegetable garden and would grow huge-sized vegetables which he distributed back to the workers' families, or sold at the market in Three-Chimneys. It heartened First Oak to see Richard at sundown, after a long and tedious work day, shears in hand, deadheading spent roses in the large square garden facing the moat. The spatula of three fingers holding the stem of a flower to apply a slanted cut; addressing it in murmured words; thanking it for its perfume, for sharing its beauty. He instinctively chose days of descending moon, to resist fungal diseases.

First Oak knows the love of the man for one rosebush that had such an intoxicating perfume. Beautiful Vita herself fell in love with the Rose des Maures, brought back from Damask by the Crusaders and much appreciated by the Queens of the Great Island. Vita boasted having discovered the inflorescences of the proud Gallica in the Elizabethan garden, presuming a new maternity, as if she had found a hydrogen connection between her nucleic base and that of the rose, participating in one same DNA. She took lots of cuttings to plant and give away throughout gardens in Kent.

Truly, nobody could remain insensitive in front of such beauty. First Oak remembers how his own leaves quivered at sundown, when humidity risen from the moat applied a moist kiss on the exquisite rose petals, waking up drowsing beauty. Its cyprine of fountain-rose meant romances and love escapes on Persian carpets. Vita invested it Sissinghurst Castle Rose, ennobling the castle and the rose in a same caress.

First Oak does not get its strong scent anymore, now that the vestal-plant has been replanted in one of the intimate gardens, surrounded by ancient varieties. The gipsies of the rose-tribe. These were Vita's love words for them. And others he overheard: they resent restraint; they like to express themselves as the fancy takes them; free as a dog-rose copulating with hedgerows. She might as well have been talking about herself as the one and hundred winds of freedom disclosed.

First Oak can relate to Vita's longing for a life of unrestrained freedom. For he, who stretches his roots with self-centred avidity, has an uninhibited appetite for growth; the change of season his only restraint. Vita longs to be liberated from the norms and conventions imposed by her aristocratic family, as it transpired in her novel The Edwardians.

And yet she has a deep sense of tradition and remains entrapped by the tyrannical grip of her childhood's home.

In her novel, she shamelessly brushes a rough portrait of the superficial and artificial construction of an upper class; the vilest portrait could well be her mother's, if you asked First Oak. His contemporaries from high up on the knoll have reported the impression of waste and extravagance which assailed one the moment one entered through the doors of Knole, which Vita depicted as Chevron in her novel. But what Vita resents most is the lack of authentic interest in intellectual and cultural issues. She can rest reassured that she and Harold conveyed their many intellectual pursuits to their sons, and that Vita sublimated the excessive reserve and silence inherited from her family, through her effusions with Harold and the way she reveals herself without artifice in her letters.

First Oak could also point out the various ancestors who combined political influence and offices at Court with the art of writing and poetry. Thomas, the first of the Sackvilles, was an acclaimed poet and play writer, and has skilfully written over 400 letters. And Charles, 6th Earl of Dorset, was reputedly a hell-raiser in his satirical writings. The best good man, it seemed from contemporary sources, with the worst natured muse. A notable incident, First Oak remembers well, when Charles and two of his cronies, in their usual inebriated state, stark naked, had offended a crowd with the blasphemous toast proposed from the balcony of the Cock tavern. Whilst people threw stones and they responded in equal proportion by flinging wine bottles at them, lightning struck the mausoleum of the Sackville within the church of Withyham. No doubt, the Earl's ancestors must have rolled over in their grave, claiming the abnormal connection to that ancestor by provoking a brutal increase in current.

However shameful the behaviour of that individual – do black weeping patches not affect stems and trunks of his own species? – Lionel, the last Earl and first Duke, cultured and refined, was a poet that Vita would not be ashamed of.

Vita has other concerns as she is writing All Passion Spent, a novel as charming and gentle as the Viola Odorata she abundantly planted in cracks and beds, rich in their Venetian velvets. She addresses in particular women, through the hesitations of her characters to lead an independent life, make their own decisions and emancipate themselves from social conventions or aristocratic family traditions. Vita refutes the idea that she is a feminist, and First Oak wages that it is the desultory memories of the suffragettes she resents, the form rather than the substance of their clamours that she rejects.

5.

The young terrier Rebecca ahead of her in wriggling contentment, Vita walks back towards Sissinghurst; towards those unpredictable towers which give her heart, every time, every reason to rejoice. Their revelation is so like the heart of an artichoke, she thinks; slowly unfolded, a deserved reward after the shadowed trenches of the brooks, the prickly choke of fields and meadows; the farmyard, the gardens and the other buildings, the like of scales gravitating towards the towers to get a hint of their secrets within. Rain threatens, brought in by a strong eastern wind. It harries the Sackville-West flag on top of the pointed roof with clangoring sounds.

Virginia causes Vita equal torment. She has been lingering in her thoughts ever since she saw her two months ago, at Monk's House. Virginia had abandoned her writing shed, the unviolated temple of Vesta to make herself available to Vita. The few days of Indian summer had allowed the two women to sit out in the garden, watching the late sunlight turning the cornfields all golden over the Downs. Bats casting a shadow puppet show against Mount Caburn.

First Oak is witness to Vita's infatuation with the beautiful novelist. A long and thin silhouette, a head carried high, similar to the white swans that parade their sinuous neck on the moat. A chiselled profile where her wilful chin stretches, while the nose is straight and the mouth full, as soft as vine peach.

How she weaves magic into life! The leaded sky over Sissinghurst is witness to Vita's outcry: this woman is a vestal! Rebecca abandons Vita on the steps of the Erechtheum and trots towards the inviting smells of Mrs Staples' kitchen in the Priest's house.

Back in her tower, Vita reflects on how much Virginia is freed from any paternal, patronizing, patriarchal authority. She is untouchable; no one forbids her to go wherever she wants. She maintains the civic fire within the new Bloomsbury where so many solemn documents, eclectic memories rest secure in her hands. Virginia has a calling to fulfil, an all-consuming endeavour. Every one of her thoughts sublimate life and Vita can only be comforted in her own creative efforts, as if her friend had instilled in her even more creative force. How she wishes that Harold knew this woman better; this enchanting person, devoted soul, so that he, in turn, would be subjugated by her kindness instead of letting his jealousy take the best of him every time Vita mentions her name. Without being aware of it, it is Violet's memory that Harold allows to emerge; the power she had over her heart, considering Violet as the cause for his unhappiness. Whereas for Virginia, who has a fragile constitution, it is the consequence he anticipates: "it is for her that I fear; I suspect that her stability and ponderation rests on precarious foundations". He pretends not to be jealous, only to resort to instinctive auto-defence mode. Not jealous? Had he not said "it is like smoking over a geyser of petrol". Why compare her infatuation with Virginia by means of such a blazing image? Vita prefers to rally what Harold had said when she had first met Virginia: "I know that for each of us, the magnetic North is the other; even though the needle may flicker and even get stuck at other points, it will sooner or later come back to the pole". "You would tell me, wouldn't you, should there be a muddle with her?"

First Oak suspects for which rose Vita is the temporary sanctuary. The words of the poem which he overheard Vita declaim out loud, her back and her left foot leaning nonchalantly against the wall of the Priest's House, had been dedicated to Virginia. Equivocal, one can nevertheless presume who is the chain, and who the enslaved rose:

Here, tall and damask as a summer flower,

Rise the brick gable and the springing tower,

Invading nature crawls

With ivied fingers over rosy walls…

Wherein I find in chain

The castle, and the pasture, and the rose.

During her last visit at Monk's House, Leonard's presence had prevented intense intimacy between the two women. Vita can't help liking Leonard for having proudly shown her the lovely room he made himself to work in. He had gravely commented about having knocked down a few walls in the process, sheepishly mentioning the pile of bricks that had landed on his foot. Their house, however, in Vita's opinion, remains rudimentary and uncomfortable.

At times, Vita's love overflows that she cannot help dispensing to persons of merit. She has enough of the fingers of one hand to count them. She has always been of the opinion that it is best to be liked a lot by a single person than a bit by all. With Virginia, it is an encounter of souls, where each finds nourishment from the same breadbin. Libertarian ideas Vita shares with Virginia, amongst which one reigns supreme: "woman are intellectually totally equal to men. Their lesser contribution to culture is due to the fact that, in most societies, they have been imposed a lesser visibility; even forced to silence". Does Virginia too resist the image of frigidity that men throw at women, when they are the first reason for it, by way of rape or their own clumsiness? That has been Virginia's experience and Vita herself had to fight off a paedophile uncle at a tender age. And subsequently responded with anger and contempt. For Vita, the loss of Knole represents the biggest scorn ever experienced.

23

Taking away from her what should have been hers only, because of a technical fault over which one has no control: how justifiable is that? If only she had been born a boy, like Victoria would have wished. Vita has lost count of the times when her mother threw this opprobrium at her. How often did Vita not dress up as a boy to claim the right to the same games as the sons of Knole employees?

First Oak would sooner choose female beauty over other human intruders that are likely to trample his roots, now that there is talk of opening the gardens for visitors. Virginia remains untouched by Vita's beauty, recognizes however the perfection of her body. She perceives her rather like a colourful specimen with the appearance of a corporal. In truth, Vita has the long and clear strides of an Afghan hound. Even though the bottom half of her face reveals her strong will, it reads like an open, sincere face and her heavy-lidded Sackville eyes are like those of a child, altogether pure and grave. Dominant, sensuous, brutal, had been the words of Violet Trefusis. An absurd contrast, Dr Jekyll and Mr Hyde-style. The words slipped in one of Violet's letters. But for Virginia, it is Vita's soul that she would rather deflower; disentangle the hidden shoots. She has observed the one thing First Oak knows is common to the Sackvilles: a detachment, part morgue, part profound melancholy. Of the kind, which First Oak knows has driven many Sackvilles to end their lives in blackest solitude, if not suicide.

Vita fumbles one of her earrings, caresses its golden crescent, a stroke to conjure the bad memories. She smiles fondly as she recalls their escapade in London to have their ears pierced. Virginia deliberately used the word "penetrated" instead of "pierced", which had titillated Vita. Followed by a non-equivocal: "I'm alone Friday night". This expedition had been more like a ritual, a consecration of their relationship despite the barbaric practice Vita saw in it. Then there had been the philosophical and historical biography Virginia wrote, in which she made Vita the man-woman hero, epitomizing her history and background. "Suppose Orlando turns out to be all about you, exotic and wild, with the lusts of your flesh and the lure of your mind. Suppose there's the kind of shimmer of reality which sometimes attaches to my people... Shall you mind?" Virginia had asked. No, Vita had not minded; she had thought it fun, for herself, for Virginia. Generously she had added that she gave her permission for any vengeance Virginia wanted to take. However, she resented her saying that Vita had no heart, reproaching her gallivanting down the lanes with Campbell, with Edith, with Pat Dansey, Geoffrey and others, judging her promiscuous. Years ago, flings, as brief as summer showers, nothing to compare with her love for Virginia. It is like a spring skyline, sometimes obscured, blinding or only a mirage; but opening the mind in a profusion of perspectives.

First Oak believes that Virginia will see through her, will understand her posturing, her search for an identity. She wants to know which allegiance she claims, Vita, the noblewoman, Vita the nomad, Vita the outcast gypsy. Virginia will be patient as she knows the difference between a flower which is forced and that for which one is rewarded at its proper season.

Vita pours herself a measure of Sherry in an amber-coloured stemmed glass with gold bands around the top. Orlando is no less brilliant, more enchanting, more rich and lavish, than anything Virginia has written before. Vita had expected the subtle humour in addition to the gaiety, lightness and accents of fantasy which she uses in her novels. In this particular one, Vita had been surprised by the inventiveness she showed, making her hero travel between different territories and time zones. Once as a man, then as a woman. A novelty device which surprised Vita. Only Virginia could understand the presence of the past which is so important to Vita. The present-ness of the past, to make it live again.

Vita read all her books, avidly, to be close to that woman whose spell she is under. "Did you feel like your neck was being broken?", Virginia had asked after Vita had read Orlando. "I feel like one of those wax figures in a shop window, on which you have hung a robe stitched with jewels", Vita had written back. She had added that she forgave Virginia's criticism of Orlando's style in poetry, as she is well aware that it is her own style she condemns. Even saying how difficult it is for a nobleman to be a writer. "The present participle is the Devil himself", Orlando realizes; "we must shape our words till they are the thinnest integument for our thoughts". Vita understands that her friend reproaches her giving advantage to the form rather than the content which, according to Virginia, leads to an emptiness in the rhetoric of her word and a lack of authority. It does not get you by the heart, or the throat. Despite the severity of her friend's judgment, Vita must smile at the way she had herself praised Orlando in a letter to Harold, and only halfway through its reading: "a cloak of brocade encrusted with rubies and nuggets, sprinkled with rose petals". An excess in lyricism, Vita now thinks.

How clever of Virginia to have seen that in most people the vacillation from one sex to the other takes place; "underneath the clothes that keep the male or female likeness, the sex can be the very opposite of what it is above". Vita can altogether feel masculine in her prerogatives and her need to impose her will on woman; as well as feel feminine in her need for contemplation, solitude, love; her unfailing bond with nature.

First Oak knows that nature is for Vita a stabilizing force which compensates for her disappointment in human kinship. Has Vita the gypsy not found at Saxingherste her very own Eden, as in Appleby, a place allegedly shaped by her ancestor, Lady Anne Clifford? Where gathering gypsies have been bathing their horses in the Eden for more than fifty and two-hundred growth rings.

Where young, bare-chested riders, force their horse at forty miles/hour, making light of the crowds along the road.

Harold only read in Orlando the immutable identification of Vita with Knole. "A book in which you and Knole are identified for ever; a book which will perpetuate that identity into years when you and I are dead". A small revenge for Vita. "Revenge is a wild kind of justice", said Francis Bacon. For Vita, it is a proper justice. She admits being very revengeful when she loves.

Virginia has immediately defined her: personally, as well as in her literary heredity. Through her shrewd, psychological pounces, she managed to understand the obscure side of Vita; a string that does not vibrate, something that does not come alive; a distance, however purposely; a toning down of feelings even in her prose. Virginia, on the other hand, has a central transparency. "She is simple, without affectation, altogether detached and human", Vita had said to Harold. She had been surprised to find within herself so much tenderness for Virginia. Her kindness, her easy ways with the children, her endless questioning which gave them a special place while she dismissed Vita: "Can't you see I am talking to the boys?" Vita is not fooled that, while being with Nigel and Benedict, she piles up, accumulates, experiences first-hand humanity for the benefit of her novels.

6.

In the refuge of her "butter" tower – as Virginia named it because of Vita's catholic ancestors and their Church towers partly funded by the faithful who earned their permission to eat butter during Lent – Vita gazes at the view from behind the lattice window. Winter mist stretches horizontal gauzes, creates impressions of islands, mountain peaks. A sky-born crocodile spreads its rangy shape. Just under its tail, a last sliver of sun dyes the red brick of the old stables with mauve and orange hues. To the West, the white cones of the kilns look like nuns in cornet hats. Vita can never have enough of the royal sight of her recovered property. It was later revealed that the blood of the Sackville dynasty beats against the temples of Sissinghurst. Her poem on Sissinghurst testifies, if ever there was any doubt, of her love for the estate in every season. Vita smiles, remembering Harold signalling in a letter that a Miss Print had slipped in the American edition published by Hogarth. "Tall and damask as a summer flower, Rise the brick gable and the spring tower" rather than "springing" tower. Unless, Harold said, "you may have meant to indicate that you had one tower for each season of the year". Vita delights in Harold's humour. It is like an unctuous, silky butter made from an exceptional soil.

Vita glances at the drawing by Francis Grose on the wall, showing the full grandeur of the castle. Sketched two hundred years after it was built, it shows the building enclosed by three arms of the moat, the tower in the middle. The turrets are no longer round as they used to be. With the tip of two fingers, Vita caresses the back of the books on the tall shelves, making the tired leather hum. Her nails are broken; the skin is chapped and there are diagonal scratch marks on her wrist despite her wearing gloves for gardening. She hasn't switched on the lights yet, as she prefers the shade that restores mystery. The books too are a dash between her and Virginia. They share a common appreciation of authors like

Defoe, Thomas Browne, Laurence Sterne, Walter Scott, Macaulay, Emily Brontë, the unreliable de Quincey and the scandalous George Eliot. They share an equal love for the great poets such as Wordsworth and Coleridge, Baudelaire and Apollinaire. Both women are convinced that modern literature can only rest on ancient pillars. "Modernism", certified Virginia, "can only be a strategic angle from which to contemplate the passage of history, the ever-changing flux of time; it is a vantage point from which to observe past experiences; it is not a finality in itself". Vita admires her sharp mind and never tires of her company.

At Long Barn, when they first met, in the early twenties, despite the denial she expressed in her letters to Harold, then posted in Teheran, Vita had seen something else in Virginia's languid composure. It had a Proustian quality confirmed by her need to stay in bed until lunchtime, which she justified by her attacks of headache. There was the limitless admiration she had for Vita, which Virginia hoisted like a sail within the group of their acquaintances. Virginia would have made an ideal literary agent if she wasn't deeply immersed in the same primordial need to write.

Whereas Vita resents Proust's mentality - the flabby impression which derived from his whole person, asthmatic, fusty smelling, only preoccupied by woman and snobbism - from Virginia she forgives that same melancholic trait. However, in contrast to Proust but in equal proportion to her dislike of masculine qualities, Virginia rejects the despicable privileges of the nobility and criticises Vita for her hereditary disdainfulness.

When they spent time together in Burgundy, Vita managed to motivate her to get up at a decent hour. Too strong was the attraction of the villages of the Morven region, with rows of vineyard that stretched their colours invitingly: purple, orangey-brown, crimson against the sparkling yellow of the trees in October. And, dotting the landscape like exclamation points, broad-hatted men with drooping mustachio and large brown hands. As the women were lying on the grass on a hillock on a warm, sunny day, they had been startled by the sudden flight of a herd of common cranes, just above their heads; the ruffle of their wings as noisy as a newspaper being crumpled near one's ear. The roots of the women's hair felt the turbulence. They had clung to each other and, like the confluence of the embossed glass and the first sip of Givry wine, they had kissed with equal fervour. The kiss had been chaste, searching, seeking a perfect footprint; the shell moulds of the lips, securely clamped together, transformed the firing clay into a solid cast. The winegrowers had taught them about the grape varieties and altitude and limestone rock; the women had shared the same interest for the textures of their vineyard plots. They had noticed the subtle presence of layers of white marls; they had rejoiced when they discovered tiny fossilized oyster shells within the calcareous soil. They had understood the connection between the hillside plots where rock is most present, retaining water, and the taste varying from one parcel to another. Their visits to vineyards had invariably ended with a tasting ritual at the proprietor's invitation. Both friends had ransacked their reserve of French vocabulary to enjoy the bouquet of the fruity Pinot Noir, the roundness of its black and red fruits as stressed by the proprietor. They could identify, bordering the subtle acidity of the white wines, the wilder aromas of hawthorn, honeysuckle and the freshness of lemon and honey. The winegrower's approval had lead to a tacit alliance with the women.

Here the old Bacchic piety endures,

Here the sweet legends of the world remain.

Confirmed in their newly gained investiture, they had wandered through a fair in Saulieu where Virginia had bought a green corduroy jacket for Leonard. Vita had nearly bought one for Harold, but she had been sure he would not have worn it. They had discovered a restaurant, as good as Boulestin in Covent Garden,

30

where the chef had worked in some Embassy in Berlin. The two women had eaten white crayfish with their fingers, bonding their dissimilarity, celebrating their kinship.

7.

   - Why do I have to take second place to Sissinghurst?

Harold's forehead has turned a dark pink. He brings his unstuffed pipe to his mouth, sucks unnecessarily on the stem. He is sitting on one of the dining room chairs; the lethargic remnants of Harold's breakfast still on the table. He has returned late last night from London, after a long absence having spoken at meetings all over the country and in France; the sudden heavy snow, unusual for November, had caused innumerable delays of trains and made the last stretch on Kentish lanes treacherous for Copper who had picked him up from Headcorn station. Harold's lack of sleep shows on each line and hollow of his face, whereas Sissinghurst presents a picture-perfect winter scene; the snow having abolished any perspective, every hard-earned line drawn by Harold.

> *Loaded with snow, and tiny drifts from branches*
> *Slip to the ground in woods with sliding sigh.*
> *Private the woods, enjoying a secret beauty.*

Vita, who was about to escape through the door of the Priest's house, is startled by Harold's remark. She closes the door, takes two steps towards him:
   - What do you mean, Hadji?
   - I mean that I come to you as an afterthought, that you ignore my recommendations and that you dare contradict me in front of the boys…who fare no better than I do in your affections.

Vita's eyebrows arch in surprise. She draws on her cigarette, her other hand pulls at the creases of her blouse, tucks the folds inside the leather belt which outlines her narrow waist. Harold expects her at any moment to bring her leather booted legs together in that lordly posture he dreads. At the same time, he envies her dashing grit which gives him morale and motivation in moments of self-doubt. His lack of sleep has put him in a gloomy mood. He confronts Vita with an inappropriate remark:

- You know I don't like rhododendrons, and yet you have planted them. They are as out of place at Sissinghurst as a billiard-table would be in the Cottage.

A light veil of guilt burns Vita's cheeks while a smile escapes at his comparison. Harold continues his reproaches, his chevron moustache quivers:

- And the flower beds I suggested for the Top Courtyard, and the terrace I wanted there, I had to step back from.
- Hadji, I thought we had agreed that a simple path of stone was more fitting for the space...
- ...One look at the lime walk, interrupts Harold, was enough to see that the rectilinear perspectives and lines have not been respected. I advocated them so that they reveal the hidden gardens by contrast and by surprise.
- This, I know very well, Hadji...
- ... and they represent who I am, do not forget this.

Harold dabs at his lips with the serviette which lies on the table, as if to blot out his words:

- Come to think of it, the gardens bear more resemblance to you: a just proportion of predictability and surprise.

Vita knows how Harold is uncomfortable when he has the upper hand in an argument. His lack of assertiveness contributes to his charm. She takes a long drag on her cigarette, the red incandescence precariously close to the holder:

- Hadji, I do respect who you are, your taste for symmetry and your vision of long perspectives, in a literal and figurative sense. Even though they contradict my own tastes. I do not censure you...only the Neptune fountain of Versailles that you wanted to replicate in your rondel...
- ... Or plant artichokes in it! Viti, you would not recognize a joke even if it was served to you on a silver platter.

- You also wanted to have niches along the north wall to display the busts of friends, of all things!
  - Exactly!

Harold's voice settles more firmly as he realizes what is at the core of his recriminations.

- I do reproach you your veneration for a pile of bricks, your unbridled affection for a house to which you attribute human qualities, when you show no interest in your friends and close relatives.
- Hadji, I am interested in what you do. I did express that I was heartened by your writing and even your radio broadcasts. How often do I not stress your probity, your thoughtful judgements, that are so important to obtain the esteem and influence that you deserve?
- And yet, you refuse the invitation to dinner at Buckingham in honour of the King of Rumania.
- Hadji, you know I am not a social butterfly. Nor can I support the farce of so much money spent on personal adornment for just one evening.

Harold reaches for his tobacco pouch while Vita stretches her back, draws a last puff of her cigarette, adds with false humility:

- I must seem so dull and rustic compared to you. I wonder if there isn't something peasant born in me.

Vita smiles at her absurd question, continues:

- I recognize the doubt and embarrassment you feel when you have to engage in another political task. You do not ignore my opinion on a function which makes you intrude in other people's lives, like a peddler…
- A peddler?

Harold hastily stuffs his pipe. A few tobacco shreds fall on his lap; they look incongruously like pubic hair stuck between the fly-buttons. Vita frowns:

- Didn't you say so, Hadji? Your function requires that you be an example to your staff. Here, we embrace gardening so that our gardeners would emulate us.

Vita waits for Harold to conclude his pipe-lighting ritual. He presses the thumb-wheel of the lighter she bought for him, sucks noisily. His face suddenly wears the air of calm and distance that Vita recognizes, as if the pipe gave him the necessary space from the mortal world and the smoke made him a protective screen. Vita impatiently pursues her argument:

- We could not, in all decency, hope that they would do their tasks if we baulked at doing them ourselves.

Vita grabs Harold's free hand, applies it to her cheek, aware of the illusion of submission the gesture produces in him. She continues:

- I agree with you, I am the sole owner of Sissinghurst and I only do as I wish; but your presence, Hadji, is the cement that seals everything together.
- And your sons? Are they of lime or plaster?

A pack of snow slithers down the roof and falls to the ground with a flop. Vita starts, drops Harold's hand, sighs, removes the butt of her cigarette from its holder, squashes it furiously in a tin ashtray:

- It seems to me, Hadji, that you are in a grumpy mood. It must be that immoral man, that Hitler you said you were worried about. I call a truce and invite you to lunch at the George. We haven't been to Cranbrook in a long time.

8.

Seated at their usual place, to the right of the monumental chimney of the emblematic hotel, Vita allows Harold to unload. He starts off by reminding her of the evening when she fell asleep while he was telling her about his different career choices, between politics and journalism. She bristled at the word "envious" he let slip in the process, but her anger was immediately defused at Harold's suggestion of picturing him riding on the back of an elephant in Delhi.

Harold, too, has calmed down. Like his face, his temperament is as round and supple as a rubber ball. He is probably right that Vita is envious of his multiple choices of career, in addition to the writer he is whose skills of evocation Vita envies. His writing has the sharpness and graceful curve of a sickle, as she mentioned to Virginia. What she admires most of all is the dedication with which he undertakes everything. His enthusiasm is that of a puppy on a new scent and he is capable of the same innocent games to avoid confrontation.

As usual, Vita has ordered her dish hastily, and absorbs the braised pheasant half-heartedly. Between two comforting bites of his well-done steak, Harold evokes the excellent speeches of Winston and Lloyd George, a few days ago. They recommended refusing any negotiation with Germany until she evacuates the Rhineland which Hitler has reoccupied in violation of the Treaty of Versailles and the Locarno Pact. Vita mainly listens, nods in agreement, but her attention quickly dissolves in considerations closer at heart, less boring than Harold's political hotchpotch.

Coffee has been served which Vita leaves to cool. She introduces a Benson & Hedges in the cigarette holder and watches Harold through a spiral of smoke while he enjoys the apple crumble generously laced with custard. Vita lifts her head towards the coat of arms that adorns the chimney, decorated with the red cross of Saint George and three golden stars. The George takes pride in having played host to Elizabeth I, as well as to Edward I in 1299. Sissinghurst can equally boast having offered board and lodgings to "Good old Bess". Vita wonders why the Queen, who had established the Protestant Church after the catholic Mary, had agreed to stay with Baker, the son. Her mind drifts towards irrelevant questions such as whether the George had had a chimney fire as in the tower at Sissinghurst, when they had to tear out the fireplace and found that a huge beam had started to burn; more smoke than fire, a fright nevertheless. Absurdly, Vita feels that Sissinghurst would deserve the addition of a magnificent staircase, like that of the George which has been dubbed one of the noblest in the county of Kent. Imposing, heavy, as black as molasses. Vita reasons that it would eat up half the Priest's House, would leave even less space in the Cottage and both aisles of the main house consist of three low-ceilinged floors, the top one under the rafters.

The image of Knole and its fifty-two staircases cast a shadow over her thoughts. She has used them all; on some she tested their waxy quality for sliding; made others resound their dissonant notes as she pushed a stick through the railings; she jumped off their steps two by two and later three by three until a twisted ankle punished her. Vita stirs vigorously the cloud of milk in her cup.

- … What is most disgraceful, continues Harold, as he makes the bone China plate ring with his fork, leaving not a single crumb of his dessert, is the attitude of the country, guided by public opinion fearful of another war.

Vita is eager to show her interest in what enlivens and worries Harold. She lets her pompous dreams slip and meets Harold halfway into his recriminations:

- What I most object to is the risk of a misalliance with the French government. Shouldn't there be a consensus?

- We might indeed comply with Germany's demands for lack of courage.

Harold retrieves a pipe from his jacket pocket, places it in the ashtray, presses the tobacco with his wooden tamper, clears his throat as if the pipe body had engaged in it and adds:

- Not that I value courage as a high virtue.

Vita, grateful for a possible intermission, declares:

- It was the principal virtue of my Joan of Arc. Did you read the critique they wrote about it, Hadji? That I engaged in personal speculations? Of course, I did! Every writer does engage…
- … You have … how shall I put it … presented her as a lesbian. This will not lend countenance to her beatification.

Vita's laugh, throaty, victorious, could well have been the same as Joan's at Vaucouleurs, just before she rescued the city of Orleans. However, it ends up in a cough; Vita squeezes her cigarette in the ashtray. She resents critiques when they cling to trivial details.

- There are more important conflicts, Hadji. Are we not going head first into another world war?
- Let us not be overwhelmed, my own dearest. We shall maintain peace… possibly with some disgrace, but surely.
- I remain persuaded, Hadji, that politics is for those who have no other talent. You, who write so marvellously, shouldn't waste your energy in diplomatic humbugs and convolutions.

9.

Vita drops the wheelbarrow filled to the brim with humus. She leans against the wall, saturated pink by the declining sun. The muscles of her arms are stiff from the effort of having carried so much load. Jack Vass will take over from her, Copper not having recovered from his ordeal and splitting headache, assumedly a touch of concussion. The silly man! Vita had to get rid of Kennelly because of violence perpetrated against Copper. They probably would have killed each other had Copper not been knocked out in the first round. Both probably having had a swift jug of the cider. Clever Copper hiding a cider press at the back of the garage! Not that she would remonstrate with them, as they had to carry her from the Tower, the other day, drive her in a wheelbarrow to her bed in the South Cottage after one Sherry too many. Copper will live, isn't that already something? Unlike Punnett whose son had discovered him absurdly drowned in the water tank. How people can say life is dull in the country beats her.

Vita lights a cigarette, her eyes on the heavy clay to which she will add the humus she collected for two long hours in the cold of spring.

Strange lovers, man and earth!

Their love and hate braided in mutual need;

And of their strife a tired contentment born.

First Oak has fed the soil with centuries of decomposed leaves and the starch of his acorns. He is inclined to think he shaped Saxingherste. Do his roots not form a ramification of vertebras under the earth beneath? Reinforcing its subsoil? He expects that the joint creation of the gardens of Saxingherste will give the family a stronger spine while sealing its bonds more tightly; a friendly jostling of mutual skills, one with sharpened precision, the other countering with exuberant effusion. First Oak understands that in this family expected norms have been relegated in favour of individuality. He recognizes the feeling of uniqueness while being an intrinsic part of a clan. For him, it is extraordinary to have been born achene, bathed in fine-grained earth, having shed one's cup like a dispensable virginity, and find oneself rooted for eternity, upstanding, an invisible connection between earth and celestial vault.

The new border will be for azaleas. Azaleas. Harold does not agree. He considers them too much Ascot, Sunningdale sort of plants. Not the lovely romantic Saxon, Roman, Tudor Kent. Vita argued that magnolias weren't either. However, the Z is enchanting. She will get her way. Between two drags of her cigarette, she starts listing: azarolier, zinnias, zarzuelas, Zéphyrine Drouhin. It is curious, she thinks, that Bunyard did not even mention Zéphyrine in his Old Garden Roses book. A rose that decided to discard armaments and has been known as the thornless rose. She will not be overlooked in the rather Byronian Z border, even with so little scent. It does suit Byron to be remembered in a Z garden, he for whom an alphabet book would not be sufficient to name everything he has written.

There will be no cosmos border, First Oak overheard Vita say. She resents the gigantic size these flowers aspire to, if the soil is too rich. She is also reluctant to plant too many annuals. She needs durability, deep rooting. If one aspires to height and elegance, one might as well hold oneself upright. These are Vita's words that touched First Oak to the heartwood. Delphiniums, she added, will stick up as a minaret rises bright blue above the dome of a mosque. Much more sensible, in First Oak's view.

Vita's stomach growls, bringing her back to more prosaic considerations. She unlaces her boots at the bottom of the stairs of the tower. Her woollen socks leave a moist imprint on the wooden steps. She retrieves a tin of sardines and a crust of rye bread from a cupboard with ceramic handles; a frugal meal and only because her stomach complains. Harold scowls at her pittance but she never has any appetite when she is on her own. One meal a day prepared by Mrs Staples is all she needs. It is Harold's company, his small round belly, his pink cheeks and mischievous eyes that exhort her to eat heartily beneath the crystal chandelier in the dining room. With Violet too, the pleasure of food was heightened. In Paris, Lyon, Monaco, Monte-Carlo or elsewhere, they honoured the best restaurants with the same energy as their passionate lovemaking. Virginia, however, remains ascetic both philosophically and in her lifestyle. Like the succulent houseleek, she doesn't need much soil, doesn't like water. Witness her humble cottage: an austerity reflected in a lack of objects. Thanks to the success of Orlando, and The Edwardians, in particular, where Vita, not mincing her words, denounces the hypocrisy of the aristocracy – and which was so successful that Leonard had to print a second edition - Monk's House now has electricity installed as well as central heating, a fridge and two WC's. Vita, by contrast, worships objects: used, over-polished, chipped; richly themselves, they express the wear and tear of time. History leaves its marks as deeply as the worm sculpts its curlicues on bark. Vita rescued porcelain sinks and troughs, now refuges for rock plants like autumn-flowering gentians, auriculas, Italian anemones and the widow iris because of the black spots on its Chartreuse green. She saved mantel piece frames, recovered mounds of stones with which she built the Erechteum leaning against the Priest's House where her sons like to have their meals in the summer. And the magnificent copper cauldron found in the pig stall, in which Merlin could have mixed his magic potions. Vita buried tulip bulbs in it; but spring after spring they keep surprising her with their mix of glaze, pastel or sanguine, as she forgot which ones she had buried. Harold undug purple foxgloves from the Bettenham woods and planted them in an old pram found among the mountain of jumble in the garden.

First Oak must admit to Vita's temerity; her feeling for colour and texture; her taste for experiments which is the prerogative of intelligent human specimens. And now, the need she feels to share her vision; her appreciation of the ordinary and her knowledge in exotic plants. What is much less sensible, however, in First Oak's view, are the horrible Yuccas Vita planted and which she claimed would tower in a vast heavy ivory pyramid of a powerful architectural value. Even great architects make mistakes. There are bridges that do not survive strong winds, the like of bucking broncos, and houses that crumble like dried peat. Did she need those cathedral spires who drink more sun per square inch than any other plant? Mexican travellers who pretend to accommodate themselves obligingly to the rich soil of the Great Island. It must be that Dallimore, surely, who only sees beauty in exoticism, ignores the magnificence of local species. The pedantic approach of the botanist exasperates First Oak. All those of the profession annoy him. Importers of foreign species that corrupt the soils, change the perspective of landscapes while Kent thrives in indigenous specimens, the Quercus Robur, so English, the honourable veteran of the Great Island. First Oak is truly offended by that Dallimore who recently introduced an American Sweetgum in the Pinetum. Liquidambar styraciflua, in the family of Hamamelidaceae, that reach an average height of thirty metres. A balsamic smell, they claim: aren't there as many balsamic and sweet smells as there are species of trees and flowers? Would incense and vanilla claim to be kindred? Would the religious sandalwood bear comparison with the common pine? What arrogance! Give First Oak the heady scents that Vita encourages for every week of the year. A Knole potpourri recipe followed since the eighteenth century, and that Vita seasonally recreates for scenting her writing room and bedroom. An unexpected marriage of double violets, rose leaves, lavender, myrtle flowers, verbena, bay leaves, rosemary, musk and geraniums, mixed with Persian spices. Like in every marriage, the mixture behaves unpredictably: moments when they exude ecstatic perfumes, the next with no hint of the merest scent. Only the garden faithfully keeps its variations of scent. However, the fault is unforgivable: Yuccas, albeit the gloriosa variety!

The smell of fish has permeated the room. Vita dips a last bit of crust in the oil in the bottom of the tin. She snorts as the thought occurs to her that she could throw the tin out of the window, where it would reunite with the mountain of sardine tins they found when they cleared the garden, ten years ago. Was that tinned fish the prisoner's pittance between 1756 and 1763? Would they have invented tins? Surely, they would not have fed tinned sardines to Good Old Bess! Maybe it was the farmers' and labourers' in a more recent past. Vita imagines the archaeological digs that would have absorbed several hours and relinquished many surprises, if without merit in Vita's estimation: rusty iron, old bedsteads, plough-shares, stiff cabbage stalks, broken down earth closets, matted wire, all muddled up in a tangle of nettles, bindweed and ground elder. The gardeners and farmers still dig out shards of tile and crumbled brick that once cohered to form proud walls and sheltering roofs.

Give Vita a piece of furniture where wax nests into the cracks, forming a protective sebum of history. Plugs, witness to a multitude of vigorous or tender gesticulations; slaving or merely preserving. Not that Vita would tend to the care of objects herself, and slaving domesticity is not her forte. She would be at a loss to name kitchen utensils. Not beyond knives and forks which she finds useful in the garden. Wood collects its reserve of nutrients, like the red squirrel gathers seeds and nuts to withstand the cold and dark days. Wood feeds on history, and objects feed Vita's soul;

are keys to her imagination; triggers to sensuous turmoil. Through them, Vita can see herself, in turn as monochrome, grisaille or mosaic. Sombre decayed wood, a bit of threadbare brocade, chipped enamelled terracotta vase, moss which unrelentingly will cover up the Ming vase she and Harold have placed in the archway, awaiting a better shelter. A fragmented and fractured image that reflects who she is. Like Vita, objects are victims of gully erosion but relish to know their true value.

Vita licks her fingers. They leave a greasy imprint on the letter from Christopher St John that she had long postponed reading. What need does that woman have to pester her? Couldn't she make do with the ménage à trois with the virile Clare Atwood who drew such a romantic portrait of Vita, and Edith, by far the most intelligent of the trio? Edy is a natural suffragette, with no need to battle like St John, who believed that the world would undergo marked changes if woman were elected to Parliament. For Edy, it is a matter of justice and Vita can only applaud this view. She is also in agreement with her prejudices against men-folk. Edy, among every virtue she exhibits, has restored the spirit of theatre by creating the theatre company in the old barn of Small Hythe, encouraging a human dimension in the world of theatre. But St John! This woman does not understand the necessity for distance to avoid falling between Charybdis and Scylla in the cause of love. Vita sees no harm in her pervading admiration, can appreciate its heady scent; nor does she resent the love-journal she kept about her; but to come uninvited to Sissinghurst, insist on seeing Vita when she explicitly told her, some time ago, that she would only concede her a telephone call once a week. The only unannounced visitors Vita would tolerate would be devoted pilgrims who would remain for an hour, talk about poetry, and then go away again. But, certainly not that of an ageing woman who presents a heart-wrenching letter filled with unrequited expressions of "flower of my heart"; "your heart is a worthy dwelling place as I like your home in my heart to be"; all that for the only night of love they had together! "Joy of my soul". As if St John had one she could devote to other disputations than her suffragettes. St John would be better off defending individual freedom rather than writing feminist manifestoes. Hadn't Virginia described her - although she interceded with Vita in the name of sacred love - as "your mule-faced harpy"? By all means, no. To require too much from a soil will deplete it of nutrients. Vita will certainly not risk being a nurturing mother for that "stubborn and sterile mule", as Victor Hugo had defined evil. Vita screws up St John's letter into a ball, aims it at the wastepaper basket, misses.

10.

First Oak witnesses the day when the gardens open to the public; the stall at the entrance from which plants are sold; the first pence dropped into a metallic box with cheerful chiming. Harold suggested the tobacco tin. He carefully removed the last shreds of the black herb with which he plasters the bottom of his pipe; sniffed it, rinsed it and placed it on a wobbly game table in a corner under the archway. People do not always recognize it for what it is. Harold feels embarrassed by the entrance fee, more like an offering which Vita fixed at six pence. Why six and not seven? had been Harold's words. Six is a round, positive number and its Latin prefix is sex, it is a good omen, Vita had replied. Irritated, Harold has tapped his pipe against the mantelpiece of the Elizabethan chimney which they rescued from the garden and placed in the big room. Does he know that in its days of Elizabethan glory, Saxingherste counted thirty-eight hearths?

From his strategic position, First Oak observes the arrival of the visitors. Eight hundred people have come that inaugural day. First, they seem to hug the walls, the hedges, then emboldened, they scatter like invasive starlings. Some pretend to have found the castle of Sleeping Beauty. No matter how deeply the poetic vibes reverberate through its walls, if they asked First Oak, he would have to drag them away from that vision. He would recount the fate of the prisoners milling about in the courtyard. The soldiers in their coffin-like sentry boxes, guns and bayonets raised, the spike occasionally pointed against reticent backs or chests. Some prisoners were routinely stripped, beaten and sometimes murdered, their brains knocked out with the butt end of muskets. George Neve had found human remains in the well that he excavated outside the South Cottage. Without doubt an upsetting sight. Fortunately, the prisoners' occupation of the castle lasted only seven growth rings.

But the worst had yet to come. First Oak was witness to the devastating fire. It took in a shadowed corner where the candle in late-night vigil dripped burning tallow; it toughened up with the rotten wood, the sunk floorboards. The yew or maple wood of bows and crossbows lent it greater dignity. The fire licked the projecting stairs of green oak, haunted the rafters, invaded the vaulted passages, gnawed on the gothic windows, consecrated the marriage of the flame and the wood in the blasphemous chapel. The one and hundred winds became the limbs of Satan. The fire destroyed two-thirds of Saxingherste, ran out of breath in the Tower Courtyard and spared the towers, the Priest's House, the stalls and the South Cottage.

First Oak observes Harold going from one part of the gardens into another, presenting his back to onlookers, shying away from the invasion of visitors that Vita welcomes. He bends over offending weeds and, when standing up, looks straight ahead into the void. What projects inhabit him? Are they of past histories about which he started to write in earnest? Are they of a future with Vita? Their two sons? Harold follows the lime walk which he had been in charge of planting. First Oak is grateful for his thoughtfulness in opposing the planting of specimen trees. The lime and hornbeam avenue continues into the filberts, blending beautifully against the Kentish background. First Oak hears him grumble under a forsythia of golden goitres, wondering what need Vita has for her "politeness", as she puts it, which makes her dispense advice, share indiscretions. To think of all the trouble they went through to create intimate gardens, now violated by as many casting sheep-like eyes. So Harold sees it. Had he been around before the decline of Saxingherste, he would have hated, like Lady Baker had, the multitudes walking around the Well Fields in search of the spring reputed to have curative properties. The Lady hated all the people and had the gates of the park locked. First Oak can measure how cross Harold now is: a photographer has followed him throughout the garden. Retreating from her intrusive lens, Harold later vented his frustration: I did not intend to expose my intimate affections to people. All she will have managed to photograph is my fat arse stretched in grey flannel. His words spilled over the corduroy arm of his seat, flowed on the Persian carpet of the big room in a cataract of rancour.

11.

Locked inside her hermitic tower, Vita struggles to write two sentences. Her letter to Harold is full of commiseration. He has recently been promoted from the back benches to become Parliamentary Secretary to the Ministry of Information. "A baby among senescent politicians with palinode-like speeches", as he had put it. Harold told her that the Germans have attacked in the West, have pierced through French defences, and have reached the Channel. Vita cannot echo Harold's worries with the agony of dirty words which she allows to bounce off the padding of her walls. She only has words of gratitude thinking of his dug-out in the reinforced basement of the Ministry. "I begin to wonder when I shall ever see you again. Suppose Kent is evacuated, as seems increasingly likely, and I have to go? In that case I suppose the Government would be evacuated too, so we may next meet in Bristol or in Bath. Would a soak in the hot springs do?" she jokingly writes. She does not express the anxiety which suddenly assails her, aggravated by the dreaded knowledge that Nigel will be sent to France. She tries to drive away those pallid thoughts although she and Harold had always foreseen the possibility of defeat, even before the start of the war. Despite her growing anxiety, or because of it, Vita's letter is short. She ends it by writing: "The only thing for us to do now is to reverse the idea of evacuation and make the most of such poor hope as remains us". She omits to tell Harold about the imminent visit of Violet at Sissinghurst. He must know nothing. It would drive over his soul like a German Panzer. She signs the letter, introduces the fountain-pen in its cap. She taps it dreamily on her moist lips.

The weapons are not on an equal footing; fear is shared in abundance. The German planes fly over Kent in long dotted lines;

some, like steel propelled pencils, draw coquettish feather stoles; Sioux smoke signals of their greatness. They discharge their insidious bombs, distractedly, as First Oak would shake off invading oak apples. The battle of Britain started on the tenth of July. And over the Weald, bombs fell on Tenterden, Bethersden, six on Frittenden, so close by. First Oak felt the telluric vibrations, as much from the earth as from human skins stretched as tight as war drums. Vita's stomach contract as the Cottage shakes. First Oak often hears her complain of stomach pain. However, she rejects any thought of death, sees herself do a Jeanne Hachette on the top of the tower, armed with the old shot-guns that belonged to her father. She imagines shooting the soldier who would dare to scale the walls, topple him over the parapet, a splash in the moat, louder than the plop of an acorn. And that heroic gesture would stop the advance of the enemy.

Vita is sure she can resist Violet's advances, and not seeing her again was a promise made ages ago. After all, they have been friends for close to forty years; her first friend ever as a child, and Violet is Ben's godmother. Isn't that enough to justify the visit of her ex-lover? How sad to have had to choose between two perfectly suited loves to her binary Janus-like soul. She knows in her own heart that dual personality is as common as four-leafed clover. Vita cannot ignore the fact that there is more to the relationship with Violet; something unexplained, mysterious, a chemical element not yet discovered. There is a bond of a legendary quality, she thinks. No matter how Vita will bridle her impulses, Violet will have Vita to herself and will be free to express her erotomaniac propensity, suggest whimsical games, while Vita will drag her in endless pursuit through woods and meadows. The wind will caress their liberated bodies in a languid dance, promising umpteen delights amidst inconspicuous sedge and travelling horsetail.

However, the Sackville flag was lowered, the pigeons flew; First Oak long followed their silver flight to the North, less vulnerable to the continent's fissured frontiers. The one and hundred winds convey the distress of trees lifted off the ground, torn apart. First Oak concludes that men, decidedly have not learned the lessons of History; know no better nourishment than gangrenous blood and scattered flesh.

Vita interrupts her reverie: does that image still serve the reality of their relationship? They are no longer in the impetuousness of their youth, the unrelenting attraction of the flesh. So many years of having been separated might have affected the width of the Channel to the point that, from one continent to another, they might no longer use the same idiomatic phrases or bits of slang, the foundation of one's own language. Will they feel awkward? Worse: would they feel embarrassed? Such a paltry notion! It came to her of a sudden: the image of Violet smeared with jam and rose petals. Vita can't help smiling. They had played at those games in the first moments of their passionate love, multiplying erotic antics. To remember the first "darling" that came out of her mouth, unsolicited and yet Vita's first endearment at thirteen; the ring Violet gave her in Florence when she told Vita she loved her. And their conversations in French for the sensuous proximity of tutoyer one another which the English language does not allow for. They will have plenty such memories to share. Vita feels suddenly rapturous. She has the uneroded confidence that they must inevitably re-unite. She slides the letter in the envelope, licks it closed; another lick at the back of George VI's stamped image. She must check on the sweet violets she forced into flower early, in the cold greenhouse. Whatever the weather, violets are the most accommodating plant she grows.

12.

A great number of soldiers returned from across the Channel, the war between their legs; only one, for some; the other a phantom-limb. First Oak overheard Harold mention the artificial fires; sparkles of light and flames devouring Westminster, the House of Commons hollowed out. He, who likes the elegance of things, is upset by the unnecessary destruction. Light reveals too much shadow. These were Harold's words on the Moat path. He let go of Vita's arm under First Oaks' canopy and declared that, aside from Winston, there was no other person as respect-worthy as her. He then went on to compare Vita's courage, alone at Sissinghurst, with his in London, which had been limited to carrying in some forty casualties from the Victoria Club opposite the Ministry. A small feat. First Oak noted the crack in his voice when he talked about their sons; both have been sent abroad. Harold then went on to enclose Keats in the same breath:

"I have two luxuries to brood over in my walks, your loveliness

and the hour of my death. O that I could have possession of them

both in the same minute."

Violet starts to fall behind. Vita has taken her friend for a grand tour of the estate. Her energetic stride is amplified by the lack of moral concern due to Harold's absence. Violet travelled all the way from the Ombrellino, that overlooks Florence. The view she enjoys from her Tuscany villa does not compare with that from the top of the pastures of Sissinghurst which Vita relishes. The lack of view had been one of the first criticism their sons and friends voiced, when Vita was about to acquire Sissinghurst. Even Virginia exaggerated the lack of view, "save of stables, like Knole". From wherever you are, the view is that from and on the tower; a homely sight, a familiar face that welcomes you. Moreover, Vita hopes they would have understood by now that the view that prevails is that of the mind, which feeds on dreams, elaborates, draws plans, installs secret gardens which open the world of the imagination: the only valid view in Vita's opinion. As Keats said: "I am certain of nothing but the holiness of the heart's affections, and the truth of imagination. What the imagination seizes as beauty must be truth."

Vita reflects that, while she and Harold have different truths, they merge at the end of the linear, formal structures that Harold insisted on; which allow to create a visual projection, give a sense of arrival, achieve miracles of optical illusion as well as leading the visitor along a narrative of casually linked tales. It is there that imagination is given prominence: as soon as the beauty of one tale is unveiled, a door opens suddenly into another intrigue, reveals in blushing blossoms the intimate quality of each garden. Vita remembers the graph paper and ruler, Benedict or Nigel at one extremity of a rope, Harold at the other, shouting out the correct positioning of the marker. Proud of his ancestry connecting him to Robert Adam, the innovative architect, Harold should have been a garden-architect himself. Vita recognizes his natural taste for symmetry, and an ingenuity for forcing focal points or long-distance views, which she totally lacks. Harold managed to conceal the crookedness that the site presented; "minor" in Vita's opinion; "major" in Harold's view. Not that Harold blamed Nigel for having placed a marker about a yard and a half wrong in the Rose Garden that should have extended the yews in a perfect line.

First Oak heard Harold and Vita laugh about their unorthodox marriage; their having belonged to each other for twenty-seven years. Vita compared their marriage to none other than him, ancient oak, bearer of so many acorns. She humbly added that she was not a good person for him to be married to, the word "wife", which she abhors, omitted. Quickly followed by a reassurance of her love for him. She voiced her disgust at having been described in a book about Knole, as the wife of the Hon. Harold Nicolson. If he were Vita, First Oak would object to the "belong" rather than the "wife" word. Do the birds that nest on his branches belong to him? Does mistletoe not find nutrients from his entwined branches, for better or worse, in sickness and in health, as long as both shall live?

Harold, who usually sheers off from emotional expression, risked a shocking comparison of his towering love for Vita with Mount Everest, of all things! How humans let out the sap of their emotions when life becomes precarious.

It matters not to Vita to have a view, just as it matters little to her if Galileo resided at the Ombrellino, as Violet boasted about in one of her letters. That little bit of history is of no concern to Vita when Sissinghurst 's veins conceal a more ancient Saxon blood. When Queen Mary and Elisabeth sojourned in the then palatial Sissinghurst. When Vita herself, daughter of Knole, has in her genes the history of a county, a country, an Andalusian wayfarer. And hadn't the ancestors of the gipsies not built the Pyramids centuries before the birth of Christ?

Their past is sure,

Those woods deep-rooted in the swirl of time,

Temples of myth and piety and fear,

Lovely, obscure.

Vita goes into wild spirits. Since her arrival, Violet has not taken her eyes off her. Vita runs, shouts, jumps like a billy goat, despite the muddy tracks the women follow; it rained heavily this month of May. Vita mocks her companion, careful of where she treads with her Italian leathered bootees; while Vita in her

Wellingtons and whipcord breeches, knows every irregularity, dip and rise of this ground. They arrive out of breath at the top of the acclivity. Vita locks Violet's chest with her strong arm, seasoned by gardening. Violet leans back against her chest. Vita whispers in her ear: "admire my property, my royal house. I am queen of rabbits' holes and Meles Meles'setts, that dirty burrower. Matching her words with action, Vita lifts Violet's blond curls, burrows her face in the scent of her warm neck, presses her lips in avid love bites; her mouth deviates to the petal of her ear; foraging tongue. Violet moans, arches her back, encourages Vita's hand scalloped on her small breasts under the pleated ruffle blouse. Violet increases the pressure of her buttocks against Vita's oppressive pelvis. The under-current has declared itself stronger than ever. Their happiness together holds in the simple fusion of cambers and curves. A perfect melding of two contradictory natures. Violet recognizes the tyranny of Vita, while she chooses lascivious but temporary submission. She manages to detach Vita's strong arm; turns around, holds Vita's face in her hands, bites her lips. The kiss opens. The pistil of tongues beckon, retract. Violet's hands let go of Vita's face; her fingers unfasten the mother-of-pearl buttons of the silk blouse, reveal the erect cinnabar nipples through the transparency of the satin camisole. Violet's fingers feel, her mouth nears like a starved fledgling. In the manner of hands joined in prayer, their welded bodies slump onto the wet grass. Violet sighs: "I missed you, I missed you."

Harold teased Vita about her being enlisted as an ambulance driver. First Oak has witnessed her flamboyant driving, her excessive speeding. So much like her personality. He knows that Harold, under the layer of irony, is worried for Vita. He knows how often she is on the road as she is committed to the Kent Committee in a recruiting and administrative job. Vita has confided in Harold her difficulties in convincing scatterbrained or rebellious girls to participate in the war effort. First Oak has heard her often complain about her errands through the countryside. They can go to hell had been her words at times. Vita grumbled about Peggy, the daughter of a shoemaker in Three Chimneys who helps her in the garden, and who can hardly distinguish between wild garlic and lily of the valley. We are lucky she doesn't work in the kitchen. These were Vita's words addressed to Taylor, the only remaining gardener.

On the first floor of Vita's tower, both women rest, stretched on the velvet sofa that faces the chimney. Chestnut logs burn like noisy crackers. An army of dusty books invade two of the walls; a polychrome Jouy tapestry covers another. The women's clothes, humid and muddied from their frolicking in the fatty grass, are scattered on two armchairs. Violet's bootees rest on the window sill. The large mirror, relic of Knole, reflects the pale bodies; Violet's head rests on Vita's long bent arm. Vita knows that her old domination over Violet has never been diminished. Violet reaffirmed her need for Vita's twin spirit. "Nous nous complétons", she said, parting Vita's fingers to count the points as she tells her why she still loves her. True, they complete each other, but for Vita, the physical Violet is more present. As Vita caresses the round belly, the full Venus mound, the thin thigh, unhesitant, she starts a poem:

When sometimes I stroll in silence, with you
Through great floral meadows of open country
I listen to your chatter, and give thanks to the gods
For the honest friendship, which made you my companion
But in the heavy fragrance of intoxicating night
I search on your lip for a madder caress
I tear secrets from your yielding flesh
Giving thanks to the fate which made you my mistress

Violet purrs under the caress of the words dedicated to her; under that, more insidious, of Vita's fingers between her thighs. Their own overruled paradise.

Hell, in First Oak's opinion, is certainly timely, now that both continents count their dead in thousands. As there is no one to cut hedges, maintain borders, depilate weeds invading the paths, and the lake that she would have liked to have cleaned, Vita claims that the first victim of war is Sissinghurst. Jack Vass, the chief gardener has been enrolled in the RAF. In Vita's eyes, the gardens have regressed to the wild state they were in when they first set eyes on Saxingherste in the thirtieth year of the new century.

First Oak has seen Vita in a rage and much distress. Her energy varying with the seasons; despair at unrelenting rain that creates streaks of tears on the heavy clay soil; cheering at the sun which peels open the first primroses.

And all through summer he must see the clay

Harden as brick, and bake

And open cracks to swallow up his arm,

Where neither harrow, hoe, nor rake

Can rasp a tilth, but young and eager shoots

Pierce into blank, and wither at the roots.

First oak witnessed Vita's moods fluctuate from the knowledge of the defeat of the Great Island to the Churchillian faith of its grandeur. And she recited Latin words, ad nauseam, like a Queen Boudicca in garden gloves, railing against the Romans: magellanica riccartonii, paniculata grandiflora, pulsatilla, rosenbachianum, aremeria caespitosa. He felt her remorse at having beheaded a delphinium "Black Knight", while she associated it with Hitler to whom she had given short shrift at the start of the war; her secateurs snapped open and closed, as if to unlock and cock a gun.

13.

There is a steady sticky drizzle this late March evening. Vita slips on her boots, her light-coloured rain jacket, slams the door of the Brew House where she has moved her study. The tower has been requisitioned for the sake of the war. The Observer Corps claimed it to be a perfect place to spot and report German air raids. Vita needs her ritual evening walk along the moat prior to answering Virginia's latest letter, which was so funny. Share with her the worries about Sissinghurst, whose walls have shaken for long hours in the past weeks from bombs falling like rotten plums. She must tell her about the musty smell that exudes from the staircase of the tower, as if oozing from the fear of the soldiers who squat it. Vita also wants to reassure Virginia that the setting for Orlando is still intact from bombings. But not from the threat of Vita's cousin Eddy. He wants to rally to the scheme of Lord Lothian to get the Government to accept Knole as national possession in its entirety; park, furniture and all the objects. The entire content of Knole of which Vita has been robbed. They will never have Sissinghurst, she shouts, over her corpse or her ashes, not otherwise!

Dear Virginia had an exquisite veneration for Vita's ancestral estate not so much for its inhabitants which the eponymous hero in Orlando refers to as obscure, but for the castle. She immortalized in her novel the apodictic bond between Vita and Knole and its history, in an infinitely symbiotic embrace. Vita has no doubt about her loving intentions which she reciprocates. The turgescent budding of the magnolia in the Top courtyard she is walking across with long strides, offers the promise of its glow under the first April sunlight; will become a spectacular tree where each flower will be like a great pure white dove settling among the dark leaves. Virginia made the comparison with hot-air balloons filled with joy. Such delightful optimism she carries with her! Even in her definition of ageing which she sees as merely soul's changes:

"I don't believe in ageing. I believe in forever altering one's aspect to the sun; hence my optimism", she had claimed. It is true that, nearing sixty, Virginia remains as beautiful as ever; her skin so smooth, whereas Vita's has not been spared by the sun, tracing fine threads on her forehead and cheeks; her skin, the texture of dried peat. Vita has always disregarded her own looks, nor was she in the least conceited. She took in, from early on, what her mother said about her appearance and does not allow herself any tenderness on the subject. Victoria had also warned her against smoking because of the pernicious altering of her "peach-complexion", that she conceded Vita had kept for a long time. Not now, not like Virginia's skin which has the silky quality, the fruity sweetness of the petals of the magnolia. Vita takes comfort in those images, the memory of past embraces. She leans, suddenly trembling, against the ancient oak tree, the last along the moat before the herb garden. With the stretch of a hand she outlines Virginia's face, as if to sketch it on the silvery-brown bark; the proud profile, the full lips; the dark hair, slightly greying and spread out like shiny seaweeds. Vita can picture her clear eyes: a tangle of stars and loose sand grains. And although her hand only captures the shivering air, the rugged, deeply fissured surface of the trunk, Virginia's love has penetrated her, provoking a steady flow that seeps through her body; a magmatic convulsion, a little death which she could not prevent. Her heart cries an effortless silent moan.

First Oak anticipated the tragic death of the Virginal Nymph. It is the privilege of individuals that engage in passionate one-love for life, to expect to be remembered by resorting to sudden death.

Now die the sounds. No whisper stirs the trees
Her pattern merged into the general web
The shriven day accepts her obsequies
With humble ebb.

However, Vita did not hear the mute alarm in her head; did not want to look at tragedy. Just as she did not want to know how deeply unhappy her love life had rendered Harold. The good man tried to dismiss the rather cruel and extravagant sides of her. Though they have always distressed him, Harold sees them as the inevitable counterpart of her remarkable personality. Vita opted for the slow shivers of passion in the name of her dearly gained gypsy freedom. She defied archaic laws, revoked prudent measures, the weight in gold and silver of promises made to Harold. Sappho always present in her thoughts.

Vita continues along the moat, towards Beale's fields. Her long and clear silhouette is like a beacon in the night. She often walks with Harold after dinner: a digestive stroll for him who tends to overeat, respiratory for her who breathes more easily in the open. However, Harold has been mostly away since the onset of the war; he writes to her on a daily basis from the Ministry. He is probably dining with Kenneth Clark or Sibyl Colefax or De Gaulle, who recently visited Sissinghurst and had to stoop down to get through doors. Not a bad thing for him to lower his head, Vita thought. That man can be so arrogant, even if Harold thinks there are sides of him which are as charming as a Newfoundland dog. Vita can see the relevance of the comparison: very tall, intelligent, powerful, loyal. She does not know about his soft temperament. Nonetheless, a portrait the French will boast about.

Vita inhales the boggy whiffs of the moat where robust stems of burdocks stick out protectively. Water lilies show open, trusting faces, confident in their near blooming. The trumpet-shaped coronas of daffodils contemplate their reflection in the black water. Can one love one's reflection to the point of losing the will to live? The reflection is the illusion of what one thinks one has acquired. Narcissus thought he was the master of his thoughts and desires and so, able to reach to his inner God. He most probably died to himself by leaning dangerously near his reflection, and heartbroken Echo died of sorrow as the story goes, leaving an echo sound long after she died.

Vita hears the distressed bleat of a lamb as she reaches the ancient Wealden fields. A baby lamb has managed to get on the wrong side of the field. The sky is still pink with sunset as Vita pursues the faint glimmer of its little body through the long wet grass. Her stride is assured, as are her hands when she grabs the lamb by its rump and carries it into her arms over the fence to its placid mother. Her sons too are on the wrong side of the fence.

Vita will happily share this detail of her everyday life with Harold, while he faithfully reports on the sombre moments of the war. The political games are too abstract, too pernicious for Vita to contemplate. She resolves to live each day that goes by as if there is no past, no tomorrow. Harold did encourage her not to worry; to continue cultivating the gardens. Privately he is worried; for her, for their sons, for Sissinghurst, for London which continues to suffer much devastation. For a world that seems to be going mad. He wants to protect Vita the way a parent hides the stain of the world. The way Vita softened her voice when she was reaching the witch part of a story she read to her sons. They later claimed to have enjoyed being scared. How scared are they, now that war has caught up with them? Vita thinks of her sons every day; for every flower picked she addresses them a loving thought. What does she give Harold other than her affection, caring and warm-hearted thoughts, support for his writing? Even though she has never harboured a harsh thought about him, she should not show her annoyance when he is around: the rancid smell of his pipe, his voracious eating habits, the patronizing way he tells her to be "a good sweet pea", his inability at playing draughts, his increased deafness. Most of all his monotone idiosyncratic whistling when they walk together. Vita would rather avoid any human noise. Particularly at night, when her thoughts shape themselves from the dark bog of her mind. Silence belongs to the night which offers so many different sounds. Harold sees this as non sequitur. He does not understand. He is devoted to the joys of civilisation which offers many comforts, whereas Vita only sees it as scary resources of modern ingenuity. He remains a city boy at heart, whereas Vita must convince him that the rhythms of trees, the unruly keys of slender reeds and the flow of the river, produce intimate sounds which are music to her ear. She can do without a God if nature triggers a state of exaltation, of rapture and even provokes fearful admiration. A parading cloud is like an elusive paper cutting. Vita finds solace in each individual bud opening like a gloved hand, all copper and gold, climaxing in the same powdery hues. Vita reads a calling to life in every bit of scenery around Sissinghurst. The lamb in her arms was the best moment of her day.

For life is perilous to the small wild things,

Danger's their lot, and fears abound.

14.

It is a strange synchronicity that First Oak witnessed the night before; an ink-diseased night. One of many since the start of the war, when Vita suffered from insomnia. She went to the large pond to try to quieten her agitation. She unmoored the small boat, paddled to the centre of the black water and started cutting waterlilies. Hercules changed the prematurely dead Nymphaea into a waterlily. Vita was lost in the contemplation of the sinister phosphorescence of the white lily flowers whilst above her head, the enemy's aircraft furrowed the sky; the fox barked in protest under the spiny broom, scattering a colony of night butterflies.

First Oak had been aware of the galls that invaded Virginia's mind unannounced; their hard core, which caused her so many unbearable frights; made her fear the lethargic state that would spread all the way into the finest veins in her brain. And the voices which talked to her in other languages, bringing her closer to losing the faculties of her mind and her unique gift: communicating her personal vision at which she was so skilled: that "jeu d'esprit", her keen wit, her razor-sharp mind. Will Vita recognize the rogue gene that led to the robbing of the Nymph's mind? She must be reassured that, unlike many of her ancestors, she has escaped that unquiet hell.

Vita will now have to absorb the announcement of Virginia's death as it reaches her on March 31st, a Monday, day of the moon, as it is named in many languages. A season when First Oak delights in the effervescence of the soil under his roots, sneezing off the white frost. A moment to stretch his arthritic branches out, to collect the rewarding heat of the sun. How could this letter, even two, birds of ill omen, arrive on such a totally bright day? However, the first, in the despairing husband's shaky handwriting, now rests in Vita's hands. It announces the drowning of the Nymph into the murky waters of Rodmell's Ouse river. First

Oak knows the small boundary between house and Ouse, the latter having given Virginia her final rest place. And the letter that tells of the unexpected tragedy, cannot yet write what First Oak has seen; the pockets of Virginia's ample raincoat filled with heavy pebbles; the immediate dive: a baptism in Jordan waters. Virginia accessing the Promised Land. Her body, only very briefly emerging, was carried by the current unloading its wintery waters.

Vita will not be able to sleep tonight. Compunction gnaws at her. She blames herself for not having been attentive to any small sign: a misplaced comma, one exclamation point too many in her last letter. Vita has been reading it over and over again. Virginia expressed her disappointment that there was little interest shown for the biography of Roger Fry she had written. However, she humorously played it down by quoting Fry himself: "I am not a great artist, only a serious one, sensitive and with perfect taste". She happily reminisced about Vita's last visit, mentioned the flowers she had just put in Vita's room. Deploring Sissinghurst being on a "bomb alley" between London and the Channel. "It is perfectly peaceful here while you sit there with the bombs falling around you".

The body, the letter in Vita's shaking hands says, has not yet been found; only her walking stick, trapped between horsetail and reeds. And the farewell letter from the Nymph, left on the small lacquered escritoire. The 28th of March, a Friday, Venus' day, that of Frigga, Goddess of love and transformation, sometimes thought of as unpredictable, who spent her days spinning clouds. "She spent her days spinning clouds" would make a perfect epigraph for Virginia who had so many luminous haloes of insights; as well as utopian beliefs.

Vita blames herself for not having responded to Virginia's invitation to go to Rodmell, on the lame excuse of petrol rationing and Harold's worrying as soon as she leaves Sissinghurst. An even bigger regret upsets her as she evokes the image she projected in a poem dedicated to Virginia, ten years ago. That of a tired swimmer, a drowning person awaiting the closing of the waves of time, her shouts for help echoing down the centuries. How long will the process of time echo her friend's predicaments?

The large imperturbable trout and the brook lamprey accompanied the body of the Nymph in her long voyage, beyond the arbitrarily determined O° longitude, west of Rodmell. Above her, First Oak could see the cherub clouds keeping up with the vain race of body and water.

Vita's tears spill blue stains on the Bloomsbury's letterhead; on the white sheet from Vanessa, the adored sister.

Vita's memory seems to be flooded with references to water. It conjures up what Virginia told her before going abroad for a certain length of time: "I'll be in Ireland in a week's time and a storm could well throw me into the sea". And the allusion she made when she received a pair of earrings from Vita: "they confer on me the lustre of a doomed Empress and my body will be thrown into the Volga". Her novels are full of images of flowing water and other symbols of the flux of life. Was choosing water a symbolic ending to her life?

First Oak knows that the Nymph could not sustain the hope that men and women abandon their reciprocal animosity, adopting goodwill, dissipating the authoritarianism of a male society. The war killed any optimism that remained in Virginia. However, she chose to go with dignity, a merging with life-giving waters, a surrendering to the powers of nature. Her death was not a rushed job, nor a rash decision; it was born out of self-discipline, rationalism, care for those she abandoned, concern for her professional integrity. Those were the qualities that marked her life. She preferred death to abjuring them.

Vita feels an acute remorse remembering Virginia's horrible made-up words that pointed at Vita's indifference towards her: "no, darling, we planted the Petulaneum Ridentis last year, and this year we will plant the Scrofulotum Penneum. Surely, she will bury me under her perennials". Not even flowers; only foul sludge, scratchy branches, rough horsetail. Vita sheds bitter tears at Virginia's words which points at the way in which Vita withdraws into triviality to avoid the confrontation of emotions. How often did she not act in such a way, burying her sentiments like she does her seedlings, hopeful of a ripening of the seeds, a maturing of feelings, the independence of each flower to live, exonerating Vita of more responsibility. The only emotional language she is capable of is that committed to her letters. She must write to Harold. She heads for the Brew House.

I have just had the most awful shock: Virginia has killed herself.
She writes this at the same moment that Harold writes to her from the Ministry in London.

It is always a gloomy moment for me when I unpack the panier which we packed together. I take out the flowers sadly and think of you picking them and putting the paper round them.

They think she has drowned herself as they found her stick floating on the river.

But today it was worse, as I felt such a failure as a help to you. I never seem to be able to help you when you are in trouble. I loathe your being unhappy more than I loathe anything.

Leonard says she has been particularly unhappy for the last few weeks and was terrified of going mad again.

When I look back on my life, I see that the only times when I have been really unhappy are when you have been unhappy too.

Leonard supposes it is the strain of the war, the destruction of their London house and library, and finishing her book, that she could not rest nor eat. Why, oh, why did he leave her alone then? Is that not insensitivity on his part?

I wonder whether you would have been happier if married to a more determined and less sensitive man. That Lascelles, for example. I know that – a) you would have hated any sense of control and b) any other man might not have understood your desire for independence.

I simply can't take it in – that lovely mind, that lovely spirit, so controlled – to think that she seemed so well when I last saw her, and I had a joky letter from her only a couple of weeks ago. I will have to cling to it from now on.

In your dual personality, I cling to the essential of you: tender, wise and responsible.

She must have been quite out of her mind or she would never have brought such sorrow and horror to Leonard and Vanessa. Vanessa says he was amazingly self-controlled and calm, but insisted on being left alone – I cannot help wondering if he will follow her example.

I do not think that you have ever quite realised how deeply unhappy your eccentric side has often rendered me. I then shut up like an oyster and prefer to be alone. I love you so much, darling.

15.

From where he stands, First Oak has a front seat to hear the announcement pronounced by the vicar of Saint-Peter of Rodmell. From his pulpit, on the Sunday following her drowning, he addresses the assembly to convey the sad news of the departure of their dear soul Virginia Woolf. His voice tries to be compassionate although there is a grain of blame corroding the tip of his tongue: a suicide is an abomination! He extracted the truth from the devastated spouse, but he is bound to secrecy, as much as possible, as long as possible.

Vita feels entrapped in a quagmire. Virginia's suicide has left a nauseating taste in her mouth. She keeps thinking that she could have saved her friend from herself had she known the darkening state of mind drawing over her. She is certain that Virginia would have confided in her, as she had on previous occasions.

Her room seems impregnated by a decaying smell, despite the white Jasmin Vita trained onto a frame, giving off its deliciously sweet smell. Likewise, the scented flowers do not prevent her thoughts reverting to the suicide note Virginia composed; Vita copied it word by word on a page of her notebook. Leonard took his time before he showed it to her, confessing to have felt like an "empty tin tossed about on the ocean". Have Virginia's words in her suicide note managed to somewhat ease his distress? Did he force himself to believe them?

First Oak hears the assembly murmuring its consternation, in concert with the creaking of the wood-benches, the rustling of rush-woven chairs, the scraping noise of hundreds of feet on the large Victorian encaustic tiles where the stained glass is reflected in small dancing flames. The mutterings rise like the foam of heated milk; surround the pulpit where the vicar, his useless handsome hands grabbing the waxed wood, utters words that fall like a judgement: the body has not been found yet. A shaking of hatted heads from the assembly; undulating veils; pulling of skirts and flounces; straightening of shiny black or brown velvet, of trousers; smoothing of wool-stockings of Sunday best. First Oak pities the vicar as he mops his forehead with a white handkerchief, straightens his spectacles on his long candle-nose. The mutterings spill over, like the rushing of great waters, shaking the steps of the pulpit. Some piercing voices dare their indignation, soon muffled by skin-gloved hands. The parishioners don't express surprise about the early death; and they are not fooled: they know the bipolar dipsomania their neighbour suffered from, her maniac-depressive psychoses. Did Mrs Woolf not say, at the start of the war: "the future is sombre, it is what suits the future best."

Vita knew the terrible fears her friend had of going mad; the voices she heard that were not quotes for her characters the like of Miss Kilman, Mr Bennett or other Mrs Brown. On the contrary, the voices prevented her from writing, Virginia had said. She lived so much within her mind. Was there ever any outer world for her? Did her mind become her universe so that the thoughts within dictated her actions rather than responding to the world around? She described the hallucination she had of birds speaking to her in archaic Greek. A dead language. Vita had also had a vision of hummingbirds perched on the Puya alpestris she cherished for seven years before it threw up its peacock trumpets and side-shoots on which the birds were supposed to perch and pollinate the flower. But Virginia was convinced that she would not emerge from each new crisis, could not fight anymore. Vita was able to listen to all that, without intervening, because that aspect of Virginia was like the shadow a person casts: its shape startles at first because one cannot imagine a body to be so large or so long, depending on the inclination of the sun. And yet one is reassured at the knowledge that it is one and the same being; that it is a part of her; that it is her.

Vita sits on the wooden bench next to the stone fireplace, vestige of the Elizabethan grandeur of Sissinghurst. The sheet of paper shakes in her hands. "I don't think two people could have been happier … I want to say I owe all the happy moments of my life to you." And other scriptural embrocation Virginia had a way with. Vita knows the illusion of the platonic relationship which defined that couple. The "moments" of happiness with Leonard, in Vita's view, tell of a paucity. How else could it be? You cannot prevent a magnolia bud from browning off in the cold spring weather. It is Leonard's decision that there should be no sex; by his decree, that Virginia had no children although she would have wanted them. Happiness was impossible with Leonard.

The vicar is sputtering from the gilded wood pulpit; licking his pale lips, attempting to bring the audience to more compassion, less condemnation, more respect for the grieving relatives. He raises both palms, then brings one hand, as tight-fisted as a bludgeon – inadvertently hitting the pulpit canopy - in order to draw the attention of the congregation to the homily which he spent a good part of the night preparing.

It is with Vita that Virginia experienced her most passionate moments; the most charged hours that fuelled her reserves "for times of starvation to come," had she admitted. Their love for each other embraced the mental, the spiritual, the intellectual and there was an added feeling of tenderness that Virginia inspired in Vita because of a funny mixture of strength of mind and vulnerability, evidenced by the many fears that oppressed her. Virginia made Vita feel protective of her. She was so like the Iris reticulata, an extraordinarily delicate, brilliant, so sexually explicit flower, that chooses the rigours of winter.

And soon the small blue netted iris,

Like a cry startling the sloth of February.

First Oak is witness to Vita's sleepless nights; her thoughts unfurling like fern fronds, generated by the nurturing of regrets. Vita reminds herself that what Virginia feared first and foremost, was self-deception, the hiding of inner emptiness and that she would become boring, hard and indifferent. He suspects that Vita mirrors her own regrets when she bemoans what her friend will never again take pleasure in. Not carnal pleasure, which she denied the need for, but simpler pleasures. Virginia will never again step on cracking snow; slip her walking stick through the spindles of a staircase; squash a walnut with a seasoned foot; walk in puddles with her Wellingtons; shake a rain of dried autumn leaves; remove the translucent skin of a boiled egg; dip in the exquisite comfort of a warm bath after rambling in the cold of March.

For both women, the simple recitation of poetry, the contemplation of a shingle, took on an ecstatic dimension where their soul had no need for words; they had a common vision of the world of silence, more real than that of language. Virginia often complained that the thought process did not find completion in words; how little words could convey. How the thought escaped "like a ghost through a window before one has time to lay salt on its tail". Virginia wanted that what was seen would at the same time be heard; sounds would come through this petal or leaf — sounds indistinguishable from sights. However, they both used words at length, in confidence and sorrow.

First Oak hears Vita's protest at the realization that the Virginal Nymphaea did not wait for the full display of spring; that she chose the ice-cold water of a dirty river, of an impressionist brown so ugly in Vita's view. She does not understand such a circumstance; a slow death, far from the cocoon of her house. Now Vita can only feel sorry for Leonard; the nightmare it must be for him to identify the ugly bloated body, and all that. Vita, First Oak is tempted to reason, death is neither beautiful, nor comfortable; he who, throughout the centuries, has been witness to so many deaths. He sees a pale light shining from Vita's study in the Brew House. Most probably she is penning her sorrow. First Oak, resorts to a lone waking.

The one and hundred winds howl in fiery Gehenna breaths.

16.

Virginia had told her that she wanted to make Vita hers alone, "absolutely, completely, for ever and then die". Did Virginia tell her that or is it a quote in Mrs. Dalloway, Vita wonders? It doesn't matter, for she inspired a great number of her characters. Did Virginia not confess the emptiness in her chest every time Vita left her? The need to tell Vita at every departure: "Do not forget me", as if she feared Vita's memory loss, or that the road between Rodmell and Sissinghurst would stretch indefinitely. Do not forget me: Vita cannot help thinking that those words were dictated by the prescience of her premature death; conveying a pre-mortem epitaph.

A good thing that Virginia had finished her last novel, "Between the acts". The word "act" has so many meanings; it performs, can be charitable or criminal or magic. What lies between acts in a dramatic play, if not a void, an abyss, a lacuna? Precisely a time when no pretence, no acting out is allowed. Then, the last act. Virginia was so not accustomed to emotional storms, having lived too much in the intellect and imagination. Would her life have only been strange intermedia between her novels, who, in contrast to her, were totally incarnated? In part, thanks to Vita. Wasn't it Vita who was physically depicted as Mrs Manresa? "Goddess, buoyant, like a generously overflowing cornucopia"; Virginia had read to her halfway through her writing of "Between the acts".

Vita, who talks about theatre, doesn't seem to know that carnations are a bad omen. The actress whose contract was not renewed received carnations, whereas roses were symbolic of further employment. Vita wants carnations everywhere! Not the buttonhole type, but the pretty scented ones. She has them in terracotta groups at the base of the tower, by the main arch entrance and has raised them in the greenhouse in boxes of well-mixed leaf-mould, soil and sharp sand. Vita claims carnations are reminiscent of the South where pots of them are stood in sunny courtyards or tired stairs. Careless and dusty if you asked First Oak. She lectured Harold on the meaning of them in Victorian language: a good luck symbol for the woman who received them. Carnations were highly regarded by Greeks and Romans. At the pinnacle of their civilization, they became the emblem of Rome, the flower of Jove, their adored God. And that Virgin Mary, whose tears shed at Jesus' plight are said to have sprung up carnations where her tears fell.

One thing Vita will never forget is how their bodies were drawn to each other without any control of the mind, and to the point that Vita feared arousing physical feelings in Virginia, claiming her lover's vulnerability, when it was her own fear she projected, of reverting to the madness she had been locked in with Violet. Virginia made it feel so simple, however, so natural. "The older one gets, the more one likes indecency", she had said. When they were together at Rodmell or at Sissinghurst, Virginia would suddenly interrupt her embroidering or put her book aside and say "enough reading," or "enough writing for today, let us talk about copulation". The laughter led to more complicity and complicity led to lovemaking. "Muddle" as Vita had confessed to Harold.

When First Oak hears Vita claim that she would have a field of carnations, from the Giant Chabaud to the Enfant de Nice and the Compact Dwarf, First Oak understands the sensuous admiration Vita has for the dark trimmings of their froufrou; like the undergarments of French-cancan dancers on Offenbach's Infernal Galop; contrasting with the sobriety of a Dutch still-life Vita sees in others, flecked and stippled petals. For First Oak, the organized disorder of their petals symbolizes the way Vita and Harold have schemed their gardens. A geometry which loses its Euclidian vision of straight lines, planes and lengths, due to the overspill of plants and the lightest prune Vita would allow. First Oak overheard Harold complain of having to resign himself to his home being an omelette most of the spring and a guano dump the rest of the time, because of the bird's nests taking over the tall climbers.

Leonard is not aware of the strong bond between the two women. Is he even aware of his own repressed homosexuality, as Harold hinted at? Did he deserve Virginia at all, as Harold deserves Vita? He wrote to her, immediately after hearing of Virginia's death; that he understood that her friend meant something to her "which nobody else could ever mean and that she must feel deprived of a particular sort of haven which was a background comfort and strength". Leonard might as well remain in the ignorance of their bond. He could never assess the weight of Virginia's childhood traumas. However, in all honesty Vita must recognize the qualities of patience and goodness Leonard had towards his wife; and she must resign herself to the fact that Leonard would have been the only one capable of saving Virginia from herself; if it had been at all possible.

She chose to leave at the pinnacle of her art; let her have that ultimate pride, thinks Vita. She can easily imagine Virginia's spirit freed from any hindrance, and her resolution as dense as the stones in the pockets of her raincoat. Vita shivers at the thought. She remembers Virginia saying that she felt in her fingers the weight of words as heavy as pebbles. Had she lost the words and wanted to replace them with stones and sink with them? Sink as opposed to think? Flowing minerals instead of her flowing prose. Vita cannot believe that she would have lost the flow of writing. Her last novel is testimony to that. Vita rather thinks that the repeated sexual abuse Virginia was subjected to, lead to an indelible stigmatisation. Her deep solitude could only bring back the state of abandon, the danger of death, that the little child must have felt, drowned in a sea of helplessness; and from which only suicide could have delivered her. Like the Peruvian lily reacting to something precarious and unsettling by the simple protest of death. "Someone has to die in order that the rest of us should value life more", Virginia had said. Could she really have thought that the world itself was without meaning, like Septimus reflects in Mrs Dalloway? Virginia strongly believed that nothing exists outside us except a state of mind. Vita can see for herself that the mind dresses up the world in variegated costumes. That when permeated with joy, the world wears fancy dresses; while sadness mimics funereal vigils. And what state of mind had she been in to wipe out everything around her? To let her "blow to nothingness", to sweep her into "complete annihilation". So many expressions of death Virginia has used in her books. How Vita wishes to have had the key to Virginia's eternal dance with self-doubt, the whirlwind of her thoughts intersecting between genius and mental disorder.

Vita's own disorder made her lose the master-key that opens the gates to the gardens in Knole. She has not realized it yet. Unbeknownst to her too is the obsession with keys that has touched generations of Sackvilles. Some have unlocked the reserves of royal access, wealth and power, as the portrait of Edward, 4th Earl of Dorset, Lord Chamberlain and gatekeeper to King Charles I, testifies. Her cousin Edy who hangs his keys from a row of nails beside his bed. Her other cousin Lionel who ties keys to a string around his waist. Keys are symbolically revered and the loss of a key might well create panic as it is associated with a more atavistic loss. For Vita, First Oak senses that the key is the last illusion of Vita's affiliation to the estate that decidedly does not want her.

Vita found her way, along the mile-long corridors, the enfilades of rooms, veritable rabbit warren: The Poet's, the Ambassador's, the King's Room. The Boudoir where she stood in front of the painting with the gilded birdcage that made her gloomy. She did find her way through the spaces under the eaves and out onto the roofs, daring to go just to the edge; she would catch giddy views of the skyline of turrets and leopard finials, and the courtyards below, all status symbols that meant so much to the family, when "men sought to cure mortality by fame", as Francis Bacon said. Oak knows how Vita would imagine the thousands of plumes that had tossed and the torches that had flashed from one courtyard to another, and, perambulating down the galleries, the Queens and Kings and poets and playwrights she could name in a litany as long as the Book of Common Prayer. Snobbish, maybe, proud of her ancestors, certainly. Was she not, from an early age, the best tour guide to take visitors around the house?

How could she? Why did she? Vita cannot help the litany of questions. She sighs at such a definitive realization: a clean thoughtful act. Although she has not foreseen it, she did have an insight about Virginia dying young and wrote about it in a letter to Harold. She clearly remembers the cold and wet November day at Long Barn before Virginia came to visit her the first weekend of December. Harold was in Teheran. Leonard was away.

Back and forth, Vita rubs the ragged silk cushion of the wooden bench. Her eyes catch the medieval tiles against the fireplace; centuries have tarnished their English amber clay. Another tile, turquoise and chipped supports a vase on a table. Vita can measure up against the imperfection of objects, and even of people; the objects tell about the life they had, show the evidence of time going by, their past value and the treasures they have become. It is precisely that imperfection which attracted her to Sissinghurst: crumbling walls painted rose and purple by the sun; no ostentation – such a dirty word - but the grandeur of the place, of its history, which Vita recognized inside and out. Each projected shadow was like the needle of a giant sundial that would mark the centuries. Her eyes move to the china egg, of a deep green colour, that she hung above the chimney and is supposed to ward off the evil eye.

Listening to her own heartbeat as well as the beating of the one and hundred winds trapped inside the rooms of Knole, the young Vita probably did not notice the scorched symbols carved on the oak beams, into the joists and around the chimneys. Carved tangles of Vs and Ws invoking the protection of the Virgin Mary; maze-like marks known as demon traps, to catch evil spirits, which would follow the lines and be unable to find their way back out; or intended to protect the building from possession by witches, susceptible of climbing down the scores of chimneys. First Oak knows that they are related to James I and the Jesuit Treason.

Vita shakes her body. She cannot help the feeling of betrayal. Did Virginia not trust her enough to confide in her? And the last paragraph in her letter to her: *"What can one say– except that I love you and I've got to live through this strange quiet evening thinking of you sitting there alone. Dearest– let me have a line…You have given me such happiness…"*
Vita can decidedly not identify with such a radical, cold decision, so completely in the unredeemable. How can one kill oneself? Vita's fist hits the cushion; once, twice, three times. Exhausted and cold, she retreats to her bed, fully clothed; tears flowing freely.
Vita gets up from her bed, another vestige from Knole, leaves the room to go to her study. She sits down, stares at the portrait of Harold that never leaves her sight. She pushes aside the pink marble urn which rests on her old desk adorned with ink rings and covered in scraps of torn paper, notes scribbled in haste, stamps, matches. Five small round vases display a few daffodils and pale pink hellebores. Vita smells them, not sure she appreciates their scent. She selects a pen from the Mexican earthenware tray, unbuttons her cashmere cardigan, listens to cooing wood pigeons in the Lower Court, starts on her poem: In Memoriam: Virginia Woolf. Her handwriting is tight, modest: a preservation of her inner self. Vita reflects that words that spring up know things about

us that we ignore about them. Virginia once wrote, "one not only writes with one's fingers, but with one's whole person. The nerve which controls the pen entwines each fibre of the body, threads into the heart, pierces the liver". Such an awareness of the senses Virginia had, and yet, such a precarious incarnation.

17.

Losing the key is pure synchronicity. Knole is no longer hers; it belongs to time; it belongs to History. First oak urges Vita to rejoice about this newly conquered freedom, to embrace with renewed ardour the beautiful village of Saxingherste which fits her like a glove. However, Knole keeps traces of Vita. Here and there, left against outer wall corners, First Oak can still see hazel branches which the brusque jerks of Vita's carving had turned into sharp sticks. She cheekily said they were to keep aggressive cocks at bay. First Oak knows she used them to boss her "lieutenants" around, as she drew them into her heroic games, clad in armour and sword in hand. First Oak is aware of the violent streak in her. Had she not tied visiting children, girls, up to trees, stuffing their nostrils with putty, and thrashing their legs with nettles while pretending to re-enact battles from the Boer War? Did she not use the sticks to frighten servants' boys returning from the Sevenoaks school; from Seal Hollow Road, through the "hole in the wall". First Oak has witnessed the intrusion of over a thousand citizens of Sevenoaks, armed with axes and billhooks, when the gates to Knole Park had been blocked, Mortimer Sackville having had enough of the careless invasion of the park.

Vita's rocking horse is still there, rather the one assumed to be George's, the 4th Duke of Dorset, as a premonition of his untimely death killed by his horse; so is a corner of the wallpaper ripped off in Vita's room, that she had scratched with a nail bitten to the quick; the blotting paper on her student's desk stills bears the hieroglyphs of her signature, exercised in anticipation of future autographs. She left traces in the many attic rooms, when, as a solitary child, she scratched the names of girls she became infatuated with at school.

First Oak, who has a natural elevated position, can recognize Vita's need for an eminent station, for height sublimated, beyond the bravado which hides her sadness, deep down. The attic space was her favourite playground. Vita would play Chatterton in breeches, white stockings, buckled shoes and a white shirt her maid had made for her in secret. She would perform to an audience of abandoned trunks and cast-off furnishings. And cried a lot.

First Oak can predict that when the day comes for Vita to definitively cut off her bond with Long Barn, the master-key to the Knole gardens will no longer be locked in the small green metallic box on the bookshelves; Vita has not put it back in the box, but dropped it amidst three thousand books that will be sold at the same time as the cottage. A leather gloved hand will inadvertently slip it in a cardboard box together with the complete collection of Balzac. A well-meaning hand if you asked First Oak; as it will enable Vita to shear the umbilical cord which links her to Knole. A perfect opportunity to put a stop to the liaison Vita once compared to that of a beautiful woman, who never, from force of circumstances belonged to her wholly. Vita has decided to sell Long Barn, only five miles from Knole; which she used as an excuse to return to nearly every day. Sometimes at night, wandering about the garden as if she were the ghost of the determined Lady Anne Clifford whom Vita admired for jibbing against the conventions of the time. The one and hundred winds of sacrifice.

18.

- Has God not sacrificed his only son?

Vita gives Harold a sheepish smile. She is aware of the incongruity of her words.

- What I meant to say, Hadji, is that I must make a sacrifice for Knole to be spared by bombs. You know I mind frightfully.

Harold nods. He knows that, no matter how much Vita has tried to tear Knole out of her heart - and he had hoped Sissinghurst would have filled the void - the moment anything touches it, every nerve in her is alive again. Did she not confess having burst in at Knole one evening, to surprise it in the midst of its new domesticity? Not quite like a voyeur but with the motivation of a carer. Harold can understand that. Did he not himself order Copper to drive by Long Barn on many occasions in order to take pleasure in the curtains of overgrown rock roses, cistus and rosemary? To remember the sequence of the gardens. Maybe to find fault with them? Harold cannot find fault with Copper, the clever man who tried his hand at making homemade grenades in case the Germans arrived at Sissinghurst.

- You are aware, Viti, that Knole is someone else's jurisdiction...
- I know, Hadji, but I cannot bear to think of Knole wounded, and I not there to look after it and even be wounded with it. Those filthy Germans...

Harold noisily clears his throat. He knows how Vita can go on about Knole and the Germans responsible for all evils:

- If you are quite sure you want to sell long barn... You did not hear it, Viti, but the name is not worthy of capital letters anymore.

Vita looks up, intrigued but thrilled. It seems that Long Barn is now playing second fiddle, despite Harold's undiluted loyalty to a house he could claim ownership of in equal parts. His "mud-pie" as he had called it. Harold lights a cigarette. His gesture measures up with his impatience. Even though he did not relegate his pipe, smoking cigarettes presents quite a few advantages; if only when he travels with the British Delegation.

Vita proposes a more rational argument; it should fully win Harold over:

- Our finances would improve, Hadji, as would our constant worries for a house and a garden that we are obliged to maintain. We would be better off without it, wouldn't we?
- You are quite right, Viti. Having tenants is not a sinecure; not to mention that at each of our visits, we must tread in like the blind leading the blind as Breughel portrayed it.
- So as not to be witness to the inadmissible way they occupy the place. Have you noticed the dining room, Hadji? It looks like they bought it from the Salvation Army.
- Not to mention the fitted carpets, Viti, competing for ugliness. You need to be injected an enema through the eyes after looking at them.

Vita gets off the damask seat. The big room is furnished with mismatched antique furniture. Each object has a precise provenance and is charged, if not affectively, at least with personal history. The lapis-lazuli table is covered with a heavy Persian carpet, bought in Kermanshah and rests on another, of silk, over which their feet consistently trip. Neither Vita nor Harold could be bothered with inverting their destination. The Chinese lamps, of a noble turquoise colour, dispense light which cuts off the angles in the room. Like the lamps, the vases have ample, languid curvatures. The objects tell fragments of a life shared: a bit of stone from Persepolis, some bass left about, Martin's latest bone, a hammer on the window sill, a tobacco tin full of seeds, a Rodin, a groundsel, a back number of the New Statesman, a soda-water syphon, an evening shoe on its way back to the bedroom.

Vita steps towards the large window overlooking the Tower Courtyard. Small mounds of dark soil are like pustules on the lawn. The vision of the neglected lawn doesn't make Vita feel more positive about Long Barn. Her back to Harold, she continues, her voice raised:

- Each room at Long Barn has been decorated to become as hideous as possible. How could I possibly regret a house that has been so debased?

Harold wonders whether her going on about the state of Long Barn, is a diversion to distract herself from having to part with it. A bereavement reminiscent of another. However, Harold has other concerns:

- What I feel sorry for, Viti, are the books that you want to sell...
- ... Hadji, they have become like a second skin on the walls of Long Barn, interrupts Vita, turning towards him. I prefer that the antiques dealers of Tenterden or Tunbridge Wells abduct them, making them responsible for the leprosy walls.
- I see them as witness of the happy days of our youth, Viti.

Vita arches her eyebrows at Harold's last remark. He seems lost in his thoughts. His protruding belly stretches two of the buttons on his green cardigan. He pulls on his cigarette, letting the smoke out through his nostrils. Vita smiles at the vision of a dragon. A story she used to read to her sons, where the dragon opened its nostrils wide to let the smoke escape. Or was it fire? Vita does not like the burning sensation in her nose, whereas Harold pretends to better smell the fragrance of the tobacco. Vita sits back in the damask seat. She says in a gently derisive tone:

- Happy days, Hadji?

Vita's interrogation weighs heavily on him. It is true that Vita's love affair with Violet, her madness, as Vita looks back on it, prevented him from being happy for many years early in their marriage. He can only ascribe to her extreme youth her successive desertions to follow Violet Trefusis, making her neglect her sons.

However, Harold cannot escape the memory of the past when he felt sorrier for their sons than for himself. He remembers Nigel in his arms, keeping his breath in, filling the hollow of his lungs, his scream needing that extra intake of air so as to move his mother and compel her not to go away. But she chose to leave, to take up again with Violet; a pact between them to never betray their love. Not even nuncupative, but so often signed in daily letters saturated with tears; poems written from Polperro or Monte-Carlo. *"If I didn't have you I would lose the world"*, dared say Violet. Was it not a fool's bargain? It is their sons who lost the reassuring presence of their mother; an essential anchoring that Harold could not have provided as he was often abroad pursuing his career. He deserted his sons in equal proportion, so many years, such a distance, when all they had from him were his daily letters; Nigel was fully able to express his grief at Harold's departing, admitting having shed tears, his love candidly confessed. All Harold can say is that Vita became like a jellyfish addicted to cocaine when in the presence of that woman. He, on the other hand, had been committed to their marriage to the point of closing his eyes on Vita's elopements, her love imbroglios, whereas he commanded discretion on his own affairs. Despite the fact that he was the youngest in his family, he always felt responsible. He has no regrets whatsoever at the way he castigated Violet. For sure, if she were to come back now, he would push her from the tower.

Harold vigorously stubs his cigarette in the ashtray, avoids answering Vita's insidious question, wittingly bringing grist to her mill:
- You are right that our books will fare better than your friends', destroyed by fire in their house in London.
- Poor Virginia, her books were like her children.

Vita gets up, temporarily banishing the memory of her friend. Three years since her death. Vita caresses the small blue and green opaline vase in which she has stuck a simple twig, declaring:

- A simple stem in a solitary vase can redeem a room. Look, Hadji, how this curly willow twig has the patient charm of Lady Chatterley's lover.

If only she knew how right she is, thinks Harold. His moist eyes stare at the willow branch with empathy.

19.

First Oak had felt the explosion before the news arrived at Saxingherste. His roots had raised in empathy with the Weald. The shouts under the porch echoed much later. The tobacco tin chimed in fearful dejection. The voices resonated along the aisles, reverberated in the Tower Courtyard. What is it, Taylor? said Vita who was straightening twigs of the Albertines at the foot of the Tower Lawn. She had stuck a white camellia under her scarf. The blandest but a strong scent. The mild February of 1944 had prompted their early flowering. Taylor, who had been exempted from the army because of his sacred disease, looked down to Vita from the base of the tower. His hat held tight in front of his khaki blouse: it is Knole, Madam. First Oak observed Vita's free-falling towards the closest brick step. She dropped on her bottom, brutally, with a heavy sigh; or was it a stifled sob? Human specimen can so easily disguise an emotion behind another. Taylor was fiddling his hat, his arthritic fingers dancing in a ring. From her seated position, Vita's commanding voice said: I am going there now. You must warn Mr Nicolson. She got up, winced at the pain in her lower back, climbed the stairs two by two. She stumbled diagonally across the unkempt lawn of the Top Courtyard, went to her room. Taylor, his hat askew, his back hunched, reached the garages and listened to the purr of the glimmering Rolls.

Vita thinks she will never recover if the vision she has of a destroyed Knole, proves true. She imagines the chimneys as decayed stumps; the staircases freakishly twisted Quasimodo's. Its antique oak doors blasted by the deflagration. Vita will spill tears over casualties among the fallow deer and sika herd. The peacocks' pride coming before a fall. She will cry over what she will have lost a second time; this time the wound more severe, the pain more acute. She implores the sky as she reaches the garages: "give me back what is mine!". Taylor, misreading her outcry, hastily hands her out the keys to the car. Vita would rather drive herself anyway; what with her tears and the worrying stomach twists. She drives through Cranbrook, her heart squashed under the gas pedal. Through Goudhurst where her thoughts freeze over the vision of charred wood panelling and floors, the marble and alabaster chimneypiece elaborately carved from floor to ceiling, with musical instruments above the fireplace in the Ballroom, suggesting music, dances, masques, sumptuous feasts galore. The chimney, surely, is the finest work of Renaissance sculpture in the Great Island.

Vita should lift her foot as she turns downhill towards Hersmonden to avoid the A21, in case there are roadblocks, endless questioning, her impatience unrestrained. How badly wounded is her beloved house? It is a good thing her cousin Eddy is not presently at Knole. Vita has a right to question his reaction in times of crisis; however much she loves him, he is in her mind as floppy as an unstaked delphinium in a gale, and he would care more for the trees than the house. Doesn't he see the treasures of Knole as mere objects "possessing a composite soul with which to rule their masters". Her uncle Bertie would be even more useless considering that he is stone deaf, even to explosion. Is he safe? Only a brief thought for her uncle, another for the many oak trees that have been knocked down by tempest winds in Paddock Wood she now reaches. Vita worries about the heavy chairs of ragged velvet, so beautiful, in silent rows, their arms forever stretched and forever disappointed.
The one and hundred winds blow fear.

First Oak knows the symbolic relevance of the chairs to past splendour and, even more, to Vita's still oozing wound. While she cries over the large Imari dish at the top of the Lead Stairs; the portrait of Henry Howard, Earl of Surrey in the Cartoon Gallery, whom Vita thought looked very uncomfortable in his very tight tights; while she feels for the Boulle tables and clock and the ebony cabinet in the King's Room and the Spangled Bed with such beautiful and delicate silk hangings that have survived the ravages of history and time for over four-hundred growth rings, First Oak knows that, this time, Knole has been spared. No other damage than broken glass, uprooted shrubs, the ground covered with thin metal strips dropped by the German bombers to confuse the radar systems.

Not like the immense losses First Oak witnessed during the Civil War, when Knole was seized by the Parliamentarians. First Oak is aware of what Vita's ancestral house owes to Charles, the 6th Earl of Dorset who was able to restock Knole House by despoiling priceless Stuart and Tudor furniture and other valuable objects acquired as cast-offs from Royal Palaces when he became Lord Chamberlain to William III. The Knole inhabitants can very well boast about owning one of the rarest 17th century collections, but First Oak thinks it is a most undesirable fate for an oak tree to be relegated as mere disposable. Such lack of courtesy! Vita, however, seems to have a strong affection and respect for vintage wood. Except for the wood carving of the procession to Calvary presented to Thomas Sackville by Mary, Queen of Scots, which is still in the Chapel. An item of tears and blood for which Vita gives little consideration, as right at this moment, it is her own Calvary she is going through. First Oak sees her circumventing Knole Forest. Is she aware that the biggest oak once crowned the sandy knoll? So high that he could see across the English Channel and recognize the banner hoisted on wavering boats and the charge within the galleons. So high that when a leaf fell, fluttering red and copper and gold, so slowly till it came to rest on the knoll, that the blue jay had time to go through half his winter supply of acorns.

Is Vita aware that so many of the avenues of trees radiating from the house - beeches, chestnuts and oaks - have been replanted by the third Duke after the second Duke had them all cut down and sent to the sawmills for easy cash? Or in a premeditated gesture of patricide. Nothing is more revealing of the hereditary responsibility one has towards future generations and one's commitment to the land.

Vita's heart capsized when she discovered the crater in the park when a doodlebug came down at Bow Petts. If Vita had gone through the northern point of the park, she would have seen the broken big glass doors of the Plaza cinema, the destroyed Club Hall in Sevenoaks. She breathed more easily once in Knole. Like Saxingherste, so much more a well-protected medieval village than a house: its many gables, battlements and pinnacles, the inner Bourchier Tower with a central oriel window and machicolations, the Gatehouse, the Brewhouse, the granary, the hothouses, carpenter's shops, washhouses. Places where they used to make tallow candles, kill sheep, forge horse-shoes, grow pineapples. All still upright and untouched. Vita, hurt and heartsick, shed a tear over the broken windows on the front of the house and in the Green Court and Stone Court, including a window in the chapel. Drying her tears, she let herself believe in a righteous God.

20.

- White, white, white, Hadji !

In the big room after dinner, Vita tries to convince a dubious Harold of her vision of a white garden. At first, she had thought the Lion's pond would have been a lovely scheme for it; it had been drained at the start of the war as it had always leaked. She had envisaged all sorts of white flowers, with some clumps of very pale pink against the wall partition, but had soon given up that idea. The place was small and sunken and had too much shade for the sun-worshipping flowers she had intended.

First Oak knows of Vita's dream of a Eucharistic virginity in the white garden, with shades of grey and the omnipresent green. As she had imagined the loving admiration Virginia would have had for the garden. Sadly, Virginia's eyes will not recognize in the virginal garden the mysterious motivations and subterfuges that Vita has not revealed to Harold as she, herself, is not aware of them. Her friend could have seen in this garden a tribute, the devotion of a valiant knight for his beloved. Would the white garden have reflected the feeling she had in the presence of Vita, of feeling virgin, shy and schoolgirlish? Virginia could not have escaped the mix of emotions she felt towards Vita: startled by her exuberant sensuousness, admiring her commanding vigour, intimidated by her patrician ways, despite the long years of their friendship. First Oak knows that Virginia introduced those same qualities in her last novel, turning Vita into a goddess. First Oak would rather see her as the dancer with the cymbals, Dionysus' follower, waiting at the end of the cob nut alley. The wild child of mother nature, despite her fingers ornate with emeralds and rubies.

Harold listens to Vita; although he recognizes the quality of her ideas, he worries, as he always does, about the expenses of a project which had started at a small scale and now seems to have expanded to a whole garden devoted to white flowers. They already live beyond their means, himself being rather extravagant in his expenditures.

- An Immaculate Conception, he says, the pipe tightly held between his teeth.
- Can you not see beyond your sarcasm, Hadji, what the final result might be? A white garden with touches of grey and light green. The whole world will envy it.
- As you well know, Viti, one's best ideas seldom play-up in practice to one's expectations, especially in gardening, where everything looks so well in the catalogues. I would not want you to be disappointed.
- I have faith, Hadji. My white garden will have the protection of a high yew hedge behind it, a wall along one side, and the strip of box edging that you have planted. It will have an abundance of opaline, alpines, agapanthus, candid lilies…
- And the ancestor-roses?

Vita erases that last contrary remark with a gesture of her hand:

- The army of ancestors will be put to flight, like the German army. Except that it will be reconvened in the old vegetable patch, whereas I would rather scarify the enemy's army.

First Oak could tell them about another immaculate conception, a virgin for whom statues have been erected. A Mary, mother of God, they brandished about like a banner. Vita was not there like First Oak to witness the large number of persecutions perpetrated by John Baker, her ancestor; "Butcher Baker" as he was named by the Protestants. He was of that species of idolizing Catholics who imagine devouring the body of Christ. He couldn't let go of his cannibalistic instinct, his obsession of white, harrying the Protestant heretics in front of the Privy Council in the name of "Bloody Mary", enjoying their prompt execution. Most of them, First Oak remembers, burnt alive; a mild punishment for a major crime such as heresy, in Baker's words. If First Oak is to believe the rumours carried by the one and hundred winds, the burnings in Kent outnumbered those of any other county of the Great Isle. There is a crossroad that bears Baker's infamous name. First Oak remembers how he felt relieved that particular evening in April 1558, as the Vampire was on his way to persecute some Protestants in Beneynden when he heard the news that Queen Mary had died; he turned back, detracted from his ominous plans. He faithfully followed her to death within a month of the Queen's.

Harold cannot help smiling at Vita's childlikeness. He nevertheless approves of Vita's decision to move the ancient roses to the old vegetable garden. He reasons that the heavy clay soil has been loosened by the vegetables and will help the rose bushes develop their "natural wild streak" as Virgil put it. So like Vita, Harold thinks. He does not oppose his wife's rebellious, sometimes boorish nature; nor her masculine dimension, an ability to impose her view, her need for conquest. Qualities which appointed Vita a Magistrate for the Cranbrook Bench. A Justice of the Peace as it were. Truly, Vita has an acute sense of justice as well as curiosity, even real interest, in people's hardships; and sympathy with every human frailty. Unlike Harold who would rather be left in peace. No shouts or raised voices.

Vita, Justice of the Peace! She knows her ignoble connection with the Baker man who had married Catherine, seventh child of Richard Sackville of Withyham. And Cecily, the daughter of John, did she not marry Thomas Sackville, thus forging an unalterable link between Saxingherste and Knole? Vita must feel the tug of atavistic possessiveness. Does she boast having had such a villain in her family, she who, with Violet, compared their respective family ancestry; which of them had the better family roots? Vita did not feel ashamed to exhibit the Baker's coat of arms, next to the Sackville-West under the restored porch.

Even though John Baker turned the Saxingherste medieval manor into a splendid Elizabethan fantasy palace; even though that now long-lost grandeur had its origins in this evil man's enterprise, First Oak thinks the white garden Vita is planning might be for obtaining forgiveness of sins committed by her distant relative.

Harold takes the pipe from his mouth, slowly starts filling it. Having taken his gesture as silent acquiescence, Vita leaps from her seat like a mountain goat, startling Rollo, lying on the carpet; she firmly presses the fingers of one hand on a low chestnut table, inducing a steady metronome-like tempo on its waxed surface, her voice crescendo:
- Almond trees, honeysuckle, white camellias; Agapanthus, primroses, anemones; cotton-lavender, white lilac, artemisia…
A last pirouette and she ends up sitting on the arm of Harold's seat, her arms rounded like that of a ballerina:
- And the Regale lilies, like giant street-lanterns which only light themselves.
While Vita is plunged in her white delirium, which in fact she sees as nothing more than a fairly large bed, divided into halves by a short path of old reclaimed bricks, Harold joins in her luxuriating virginal vision. He tenderly strokes his wife's peppered dark hair. Harold vividly remembers the straight thick mane on young Vita's shoulders at a time when he and his family had been conveyed to visit Knole. Long bohemian hair which suited Vita's wild streak perfectly. He pats Vita's hand lightly before striking a match to light his pipe and ventures, not without irony:
- They are risky marriages…However, I can see a central harbour where white roses would climb…
- The rampant Mulliganii, Hadji. I have foreseen four of them.
- And a bench for me to sit on?
- Your back to the yew hedge, Hadji, where you can have a nap in contemplation of the Regale lilies, their white trumpets

resounding through the grey of southernwood and artemisia and silver santolina. And your hand will stroke the velvety Rabbit's Ears…
- Or bear's ears…
- … As the French say. Not everyone speaks Latin.
- Or lamb's ears, depending on the soil you come from.

Harold takes three short puffs before laying his pipe on the alabaster ashtray.
- Talking of silver, Viti, how will you pay for those expenses?
- Don't trouble my marriage blanc, Hadji.
- Dear Viti, you seem to dream your white garden as large as the flat I share with Nigel and Ben in Kensington.
- I am aware of the sacrifice you made giving up your flat in The Temple, Hadji.

Vita gets up from the arm of the seat, kisses Harold's balding head:
- Other times, other dreams, Hadji. But we are dreaming together, aren't we?

She takes three steps to leave the room, pushes her head through the door before closing it:
- Have I shared my vision of the great ghostly barn-owl silently sweeping across the pale garden, in the twilight? Pure mimesis, Hadji.
- And desire, I should think? Are you sure, Viti, you are not confusing it with the ghost of Lady Anne Clifford?
- She would have had a prayer book in hand. Believe me, Hadji, Knole is now a prehistoric animal. You admire its powerful impact but you would not want it as pet, would you?

It is not just the white owl that will frighten at twilight. First Oak prophesises that the almond trees that Vita intends to plant in the white garden will have reason to fear the cunning roses which will steal away the light as fast as a cloud shrouds the sun. Not least because Vita is light-handed when it comes to pruning climbers. No head shearing, no systematic pruning. If she bends the stems of the Mulliganii, which are surprisingly docile, she will leave them every freedom to jaculate; likewise, her own liberty.

No matter what, First Oak persists in seeing a simplicity to Vita; the white she craves would echo that which she saw during her first visit at Saxingherste. A month of April of spring renewed, saturating with white everything around the ruins: cherry trees, plum trees, pear trees, hawthorn. A whitening of orchards and row hedges. The new-born lambs rollicking on beds of daisies and cuckooflowers. A quintessence of purity and innocence. First Oak is of the opinion that white is written all over Vita like a white page where she can rewrite history, appropriate the inheritance of Knole, a just revenge for having been dispossessed of it for a mere gender mistake. Might the white garden be that stretch of light in her life as she talks about it as a morass, a bog, a swamp, a deceitful country?

21.

- I thought I would have lost all pleasure in the lake, Hadji, or indeed even our woods.

Harold and Vita are having an inspection tour around the estate. They walk through the woods which give off the unpleasant smell of cooked onion from the decayed wild garlic. They reach the lake which had given Vita the ecstatic feeling of having reconquered her despoiled heritage. After the war, Vita had told Harold that she would never love the lake and the woods again in the same way she used to, since the soldiers came and tarnished them with their leather boots and pickaxes, scattering the paths with cigarette butts and phlegm. Did she imagine some pissing in the lake or against the tender bark of silver poplar? Their insolent and loud guffaws? On par with the tanks that came into their woods bruising the young tender oaks. When they finally took their leave at the end of the war, they had been replaced by a noisy bus service between Biddenden and Cranbrook, skirting their wood. The war has had many pernicious consequences. However, they should be grateful for the safe return of their sons.

First Oak saw their sons returning from the war along the newly tarmacked road; as black as death itself, as shiny as silver-headed nails. Benedict, in his British Army officer uniform, having been wounded but free and without plaster, as Vita put it. The Sackville flag had been displayed on the tower at the end of the war, and it hung again on Wednesday the 4th of June 1952, for the visit of the Queen Mother at Saxingherste. Vita deployed a skirt for the occasion, revealing her elegant reed-like legs. The royal visit was a recognition of Vita's thirty-five years of gardening and love for the plant kingdom. She can rely on Jack Vass again, a gardener close to her heart, she says. Besides, so good looking, so decorative. Vita, not wearing her heart on her sleeve, uses her sentiment for the gardener as a veil of deception for her most comforting affections; for Harold, for her sons.

Vita and Harold cross the sheep pastures, starting the donkey Abdul's braying, sheep scattering, and reach the main alley to Sissinghurst.
- The shock absorbers no longer suffer from the bumps and potholes of the lane, Hadji. Wouldn't that be called a truce?
- Don't trivialize the war now that our sons are safely back, Viti.
Harold suddenly stops in the middle of the lane, raises his head towards the tall tree alongside it:
- Look Viti, how the horse-chestnuts are beginning to light their candelabra. The sad patience of the lighthouse, he adds.
Vita is struck by his tone of voice.
- It is beautiful, Hadji, who wrote this?
- Pierre Loti, maybe?
- It could have been Virginia, Vita says.
She gives the gate to the herb garden a brusque push; Harold's silence is thick. Vita is neither a cook, nor an herbalist, but she recommends growing a large variety of herbs, familiar or strange, to maintain rich contrasts of colour and texture of leaves and flowers. Lavender for its scent, the compass-rose of fluffy cotton, the hyssop that bees delight in, calendula which is synonym of sun for Vita, the star-shaped dill, the blue rosemary flowers, and many other herbs that give off their scents on this June day.

Tansy, thyme, Sweet Cicely,

Saffron, balm, and rosemary

That since the Virgin threw her cloak

Across it, - so say cottage folk –

Has changed its flowers from white to blue.

- Our garden is mellow and warm and welcoming and a haven of peace, Harold says, with the satisfied tone of a new proprietor.

Now that he spends more time writing, Harold seems to have reclaimed Sissinghurst. To Vita's greatest satisfaction as it had been her idea of heaven on earth for Harold to be more often near her. Also because she believes in his writing and always regretted that by force of circumstances he regarded it as a side-line. Vita crumples a lavender spike between her fingers, rubs the back of her ears.

- Our gardens, Hadji, are an oasis of beauty in a world that is too often indifferent to poetry.

First Oak overheard Vita confiding to Harold her disappointment and deep sorrow for having been excluded by the Poetry Committee of the Society of Authors. It had been a blow to her sense of self, she said. Harold could only empathize with her; even more so because she had also been excluded from Denys Kilham Roberts' anthology of British poetry as well as been overlooked at a Wigmore Hall poetry reading in the presence of the modest ears of the Princesses Elizabeth and Margaret. Enough to turn your entrails into a knot, as First Oak knows to compare it with the consequence of desiccation of the tissues when an injury is inflicted. The progressive death of cells, chemical modification; the impregnation of the membranes and sealing of vessels by various substances. Containing no living cells, the wood changes its colouring, its density.

Vita's injury is of this nature. She aspires to renown for her poetry; the only thing that makes her truly and completely happy, she said. First Oak is aware that the stopover of the recently widowed Queen was a most comforting balm for Vita. She needs signs of recognition like as many kisses to Sleeping Beauty, reviving her, propelling her into new projects, again and again, in culture with words or cultivation of new plants.

Vita, who counts poets among her ancestors; who dined with prominent poets and takes pride in the collection of Restoration poets and playwrights at Knole. Millais' painting of Saint Agnes, based on Keats' poem sets the scene in the King's bedroom at Knole. Had Vita not found some affinity with the Poet Laureate Robert Bridges with whom she discussed prosody during long hours at his house near Oxford? He who, at over eighty years old, sitting on a blanket on the grass and reading the proofs of The Land, praised Vita for her Virgilian bite. No one else but Vita could argue with a man of such strength of expression, altogether precise and delicate, on the number of vowels in a verse, on the metrics needed to balance out syllables, accented or unstressed. Had she not learned as much from the Virginal Beauty whose purity equalled her restraint? Likewise, in First Oak's view, Vita achieved a just harmony of shades, of necessary accentuation in her gardens.

22.

Vita and Jack Vass have worked so hard to prepare the gardens for the British Fair. On this June day, it looks its best; in particular Vita's favourite summer-flowering roses which she considers having a generosity that is as desirable in plants as in people.

- The joy of a rose is in such a June evening as it is now, Hadji, when once in a while we are allowed to enjoy a deep warm sloping sunlight.

Vita is grateful for Jack's return after his long years in the RAF. "The gardens must show their splendour for the British Fair", he had said. "In their best possible light", Harold had confirmed from the BBC's Overseas Service, where he continues his broadcasts on Foreign Affairs. The days are gone when he would resent and shy away from any intrusion in the gardens. He even authorized the BBC to film a documentary of Sissinghurst.

- People always want more, Vita suddenly says. Despite Attlee's welfare state which will take care of the population from cradle to grave, as the Labour Party puts it.
- True, the establishment of the NHS is the Labour Party's most important achievement, Harold says, with a touch of pride and regret nonetheless.

He has finally put an end to his political ambitions since he failed to win the seat in the Labour Party at the 1945 election and lost a by-election in North Croydon three years later. And a good thing too, as Vita thought it awkward that Harold should be Labour while Nigel was standing as Conservative candidate in Leicester.

Vita stubs out her cigarette in a small saucer near a leg of the bench in the white garden; Jack or any other helping hand will empty it while doing the inspection of the gardens. Harold has plonked himself down on the bench with a heavy sigh. Vita casts an endearing look at Harold, who, at soon sixty-six - the mark of the beast as himself put it - is still active and, like her, prolific in his writing. They are both aware that they equally hate the fact of ageing. Not just for the superficial reason of the physical aspects mentioned by Harold in a letter; that one gets fat and bald and tutti quanti. But for Vita, who overlooks her persistent back and stomach pains, the real deep reason is to know that they have only twenty or thirty years to live; that they hate the idea of leaving Life as they both love it and enjoy it. To disavow and delay ageing is a necessity, Vita thinks, as there is such an immense background of ideas that ought to get down on paper. And the grandchildren are soon to be, now that Nigel and even Benedict are married - which for the latter came as a surprise as Harold always suspected his homosexual inclination. Luisa is such a love understanding the deep nature of Ben, having seen the gold in him despite his difficult character. He can be altogether quicksilver and leaded, humorous and solemn. Neither Vita nor Harold would ever be able to classify him, if it was at all necessary. So much like her, so much the way she created a mix of emotions in the garden, with big or delicate planting, daring or careful, a rampageous jumble refuting any idea of conventional patterns.

Harold just completed the biography of George V, that Vita so enjoyed reading and was impressed with. She had put a reservation however, on the fact of Harold getting a bit too frightened of what he regards as the "too personal touch", thus denying his own special gift, abjuring his own genius.

She is not quite satisfied with her latest novel "Devil at Westease", an absurd thriller story she embarked on for an American magazine and for which she was paid three-thousand pounds. It had been written in four weeks, interrupted by the guidebook to Knole that the National Trust commissioned her to write, rekindling her sorrow, costing her phases of discouragement when what she read about her murder story seemed vile in comparison, then corrected or torn up; had her good nights and bad mornings and the other way around, hopefully compensated by moments of exaltation that her memory could list every object in every room at Knole. Her heart, however, closed on by rodent's teeth.

Knole excepted, the lack of recognition for Vita's poetry must have been the biggest blow she ever suffered. She had to content herself with the Heinemann prize of the Royal Literary Society for her novel The Eagle and the Dove. Vita has gone all religious in her piece of writing about two saints. One she compares to an eagle, the other to a dove. Contrasting portraits First Oak would not hesitate to say Vita herself embodies. The Spanish Avila, a woman of beauty, breeding and culture, energetic, resourceful; the little Lisieux flower, all gentleness and wishing to live a cloistered life.

Vita also obtained medals from the Horticultural Society and she could also take pride in having been appointed a Companion of Honour for her services to literature and having received the Hawthornden price for her poem The Land.

"The poem can wait", T.S. Eliot said. However, for Vita nothing is less certain. Writing makes her febrile. If she wakes up in the middle of the night with an idea, as First Oak often witnessed, she must immediately put it down into words.

Vita picks up the conversation where they left off:
- Even so, Hadji, are we headed towards a better world with the levelling of social classes and the disappearance of the privileges of the nobility?
- A classless world as the young Tories want it, Harold says, not without irony.

Vita sits down next to Harold, lights another cigarette. Her sigh is diluted with the first puff; her eyes follow the white plumes of smoke rise in the light hot air. So much like their partnership, she thinks: a fusion of two impalpable lightnesses, one vital, the other toxic. Could she have been that arsenic particle in Harold's life?

She pushes away the intrusive thought. After all, did she not largely compensate her shortcomings of the first years of their marriage?

- Most people are ignorant of a simple alchemy, Hadji. Which is to give attention in order to receive ten or twenty times more in return.

Harold doesn't reply. His eyes are fixed on the entanglement of the Mulliganii roses that have been so impetuous as to choke the almond trees. Vita has put a lot of herself in this garden, he thinks, while Vita continues:

- It seems to me that the population demands a great deal but is reluctant to shoulder any civic responsibility, don't you think?

Harold has his eyes closed. He very often falls asleep in the middle of a conversation. Vita doesn't take offence. Harold is aware of her convictions.

For Vita, as First Oak has been witness of it for the past twenty years, her first responsibility is for her gardens. She must preserve an inheritance that was entrusted to her. He knows how Vita feels in osmosis with her plants. She incubates the seeds like one does for young animals, giving them shelter and biological, parental protection. She takes the time to watch them grow, encouraging them with doses of love and appropriate nutrients and, moreover, by respecting their growth rhythm.

Vita leaves the bench, the quietness of the white garden and Harold who deserves a short nap before the intrusion of visitors. As she stands at the foot of the tower, she reflects about how important the tower at Knole had been, where she had her secluded room. She fared no better in the tower than seedlings in a cold greenhouse. Her mind is drawn back to the shelter of the attic rooms where she gave free reign to her dreams and her creative frenzy; in the rolling ancient park where she practiced her games in khaki and armour; scattering the clumps of fallow deer, imagining Queen Elizabeth and Philip Sidney pursuing them; as if she wanted to claim prerogative power on the domain; when the gypsy in her thought the whole earth was hers. However, she is well aware that a major ingredient was missing in her nurturing: the love of her mother. Even if her father did not understand her complicated personality and wished for her to be "normal", the relation with him was like a rich compost, filtering, full of nutrients, while that with her mother, Harold went as far as saying, that Victoria often got the wrong substrate, even the wrong pesticide: "substituting Mercury salt for wormwood manure", as it were. The comparison was justified if Vita adds up the number of times her mother threatened her, temporarily disinheriting her, requesting that she give back some family jewellery, calling her "the Vipa" as in viper, uttering insults and other "postilions weather of language", as Jules Renard put it. It has been sixteen years since her death and no, her daughter does not regret her at all. Her father yes, this alluring blood horse "whose life has proved too much for him", as Virginia said.

Vita lights a cigarette. The memory of her mother is intrusive on such a nice peaceful day. The smoke temporarily covers the delicate scent of the roses, to the right of the stairway down the tower. Three Albertine, of a pale pink, rare among the rambling wichuraianas, and a Paul's Lemon Pillar, with white flowers. Not quite white, but greenish, suffused with sulphur-yellow; the perfection of their form: each bud of the Lemon Pillar has a sculptural quality which suggests curled shavings of marble, if one may imagine marble made of the softest ivory suede. Vita will share these thoughts in her article for the Observer. Like so many climbers on the walls of Sissinghurst, Vita had planted them even before they had signed the contracts for its acquisition, staking out her territory. Vita admires how both climbers merge together, letting their heart. They now form a huge flowering tapestry against the red bricks. The Lemon Pillar being a bit more reluctant to be trained. Is that not the essence of her relationship with Harold? The encounter of two identical spirits, twinned souls;

one bendy and easy, one rebellious. Those two ramblers are her favourites; even if Hidcote Yellow was recently nominated by the RHS; even though Madame Alfred Carrière will flush pink from envy; even if the Mermaid is the one rescuing other climbers when they are past their best. The more so because the Mulliganii have terrorised the almond trees, swathing them in a fragrant curtain, the trees collapsing under the weight of the rose. However, Vita loves roses for giving back so much more than the work and care they require. They have a prodigality of spirit, producing flowers with much enthusiasm. Give Vita the exuberance of roses and stick to the first rule which is to prune them quite loosely.

Vita is drunk on roses, accepting their whims and sharp thorns, while she despises the *Carduus* specimens she compared her mother to. First Oak can appreciate the rash judgment as he himself is surrounded by their burdock relatives. How they dare their stingers on rabbits and badgers! Even Vita's dogs had a brush with those prickly beards; the ingestion of some seeds caused irritation of their guts. Their canine faithfulness leads them to utter symbiosis with Vita, who day after day complains of Pyrosis. As if the fire of wrath burned her entrails.

The rose garden offers a vivid contrast with Knole where her mother would grow spaced out rows of midget roses in a mix of loud colours, savagely pruned, in parallel, which, by definition, never intersect. Never any scent at nose's height, never a carpet of petals to walk on. A sanitized garden lacking generosity, probity; only reflecting a stupid convention similar to the unused greenhouses, the orangeries, the rhododendrons, an army of yews as wide as the Hastings' pier, that encapsulated their own emptiness and the pretension of their creators. The portrait of Victoria who was keen to listen to Gertrude Jekyll's advice rather than recognizing the flair her daughter had for gardening.

First Oak has no doubt that Vita's priorities lie with her gardens rather than poetry. Her gypsy blood boiled over and the £ 100 Heinemann prize money was spent on more azaleas and red-hot pokers which Harold detests. The love of nature has attained the proportions of a vice, she wrote for the New Statesman. Nature moves her to a sense of wonder, awe and comfort. The Weald an antidote, alkali on acid.

However, the one and hundred winds ring a death halloo.

23.

Harold seems to have a sense of happiness, like some have a sense of humour. Unlike Vita who has neither. For her, happiness lies in small instantaneous occurrences. Yesterday for example, at sunset, as she was crossing Horserace field with Rollo, the Alsatian, she had had cause for enchantment watching the lambs playing a game around a big oak. They scampered round and round after each other, and again; and sometimes butted each other when they caught one another headlong. They even tried to run up the trunk of the oak, and then fell off and ran around again. A brief suspended moment of wild happiness, ignoring back and stomach pains, Rollo panting at her side, evidently spellbound.

The cabrioles of the young animals, their impetuous escalades reflect Vita's own seeking of strong sensations in her libertine encounters. What motivated her need for ephemeral trespassing? What did the light-heartedness of her sexual encounters do for her other than confirming the life-giving quality of flesh? Now, only the passage of seasons in the garden rewards her with life in the full; as well as death.

The sickness which entered her is a throbbing reminder of it. First Oak knows how important it is to incise deep into the wood to remove as much of the canker fungi from the tree. Verify that the sick bit remains clean, a clear cut, Pam Schwerdt, the new head gardener recommended; make cuts through the fibres in the most inner part, until the wound is completely sealed. To prevent humidity stagnating in the fibrous bits. It is First Oak's opinion that Vita's cancer drank from stagnating tears and ill-humours. Why did she not fully voice her resentment and anger in the face of the most serious amputation she was inflicted? Her adored Knole, her most inner part; her wound never completely healed. First Oak could tell her that it is often the environmental conditions which are responsible for tree cankers. Too heavy soils or underground water, even the stress of trampled roots. Isn't that what happened to Vita's? In the worst cases, Pam had said for an old pear tree in the orchard, you bite into its last fruits and cut it down.

Vita knows all too well the humiliation of dying. Her father left with hardly any skin on his bones, the shame of his degradation present in his eyes. Not the "distinguished thing" Henry James worded as he felt death closing in. what Vita wishes for herself is neither distinguished nor humiliating, but a simple moment where she can still bite into a fruit, standing; and hope for a transubstantiation effect.

Vita bites into life right now as spring imposes itself as of right; as she threads onto the thick carpet of sorrel and buttercup-sprinkled grass; as the white and pink blooms of the orchard open in Eucharistic offerings; their flowers about to reveal their fruit in a slow undress. Vita feels like she has the power to extract every micron of pleasure, taste the full flavour of life. Nature is her religion. She wants every sign of life to resist her heretic thoughts of death. Not so much her own death as that of her loved ones. She recently lamented in a letter to Harold at the prospect of his dying. Don't let him go before her, she invokes the fleece-speckled sky of this April morning.

And I shrank from the English field of fritillaries

Before it should be too late, before I forgot

The cherry white in the woods, and the curdled clouds,

And the lapwings crying free above the plough.

Why must she have the awful thought of his death when she has just observed Harold tending to his morning ritual, peering into the hollowed stone in the Cottage Garden with his rain gauge. Such a comforting futile gesture, so touching the blue coat and black hat and yet reduced vision from the window of the tower. The sort of sudden view of a person one loves that makes you want to open the window and cry: I love you. Did she do it, did she say it? If she were to die here, now, would she have told Harold enough that she loves him? "How one does love the odd corners of people whom one loves", Harold had said.

First Oak is aware of the tender concern Vita felt for her gardens, less so for herself! Vita only allowed herself to express her feelings for those she loved within the limits of respect and recognition for who she was. First Oak can now see how deep the love she has for her three men, her grandchildren; her lasting friendship with Virginia.

Responsible passion she expressed for an estate that will continue to be a tribute to her immense ingenuity.

How odd to think that the true love for Harold has survived and improved with time, whereas her passion for Violet Trefusis has dried out like a Wâdi in wait of the rainy season. Vita has long ago lost the imperious need of the flesh; after renouncing her passions, the more so after Virginia's death, she had become satisfied with the serenity, the companionship. She became aware that what made her happy was the more profound and more lasting love she had found with Harold, the "odd fish", as he calls himself. Oh, that he would be spared another stroke! That she could have read the signposts of her own sickness. Or had she? Her last book written during a cruise to the West Indies, in which Edmund Carr is told he has only a few months to live, bears it in its title. How many more seasons for her?

Vita has lost the battle against trespassing cancer cells. First Oak regrets that science ignores that the saprophyte fungi which grows on the Japanese Oak could have cured her cancer. Likewise, the tendril-bearing vine of the balsam-pear or even the graviola fruit which Vita would have grown in her garden, had she known. Middle-aged spread has begun with battles against nettles and thistles. How many more seasons will Vita's hand crumple up the evergreen myrtle's pointed, dark-green leaves, against the wall of the Big Room. She relishes its lemony fragrance on her fingers. How many more fruit will it sacrifice to flavour the Sunday lamb roast Vita prefers? Its flowers of a delicate white and gold smother the bush in a way that it appears a cloud of butterflies has landed on it, as Vita sees it.

This new season will bring back her grandchildren Juliet and Adam. How enjoyable to hear the little tap dancing steps of the children as they follow her through the garden. Vita is not sure how to show warmth and love, even an encouraging hand, in particular with shy Juliet. Other than sharing her knowledge around the farm; other than giving them the measure of the country habit that has her by the heart. Her grandchildren in turn will have to prevent Sissinghurst from losing its soul, its inner grandeur, as Vita fears that her baby will be taken away from her; the Trust or any other foreign body. Not as long as she lives, but later, irrevocably. The evisceration will be subtle. She fears that the farm will go first.

Haymaking, baling, silage, sheep shearing, lambing season, fruit harvesting and cider making. The perfume of apples wafting in silent penitent procession, invading every room. In the busy weeks of hop-picking, their delight in the bitter-sweet smelling inflorescence. "So like artichokes", Juliet had rightly ventured. The children love to sit around the campfires with scores of East End pickers chatting in their cockney slang, drinking their tea; fortunately, the smell of the fire covers that of the detestable beverage. Another hated habit which Vita wanted to spare the children: the dogs let lose to grip the rats running from the barn, shaking their bodies to death while the men joke and hide their scorn behind the smoke of their rolled cigarettes.

First Oak wonders how many more seasons will Vita sample the Rosa gallica, as she would generously stir red cherry juice into a bowl of cream. Will she see the Nevada flower twice, in June and again in August, a snowstorm in summer, as her name implies? And the Moss rose, like embroidered cushions, unravel its trimmings similarly to those in Vita's room; and the pear-shaped ghost of Madame Plantier, in her efforts to look both matronly and virginal.

How many more seasons will Vita complain about the sparrows pecking the buds off the Corylopsis pauciflora? Her captivation in hearing the young owls hiss in their nest over the cowshed; her delight in the rosa filipes adorning the old pear tree of its Alençon needle lace, a tangle of elegant knobs and gaps. And her beloved gypsy roses of which Vita celebrates the immense freedom; how long will she be able to contemplate the mirror of their Persian textures in which she says she could find the velvety sensations and the colours of the carpets sold on the markets of Isfahan, Bokhara and Samarkand?

Will she still see the abutilon dancing for Madame Alfred Carrière on Prince Igor's closing chorus; the petticoat of its yellow petals that spring out in flares, rotate on the point of the stamens.

Will she stretch the seasons to see the tender butter-yellow Coronilla glauca hyphening between Christmas and Easter, linking the Birth and the Resurrection, as Vita says. Its strong scent still takes you by surprise by day, is however absent by night.

Will spring return with the hooded meadow fritillary, which Vita loves more than any spring bulb. A sinister little flower in its mournful colours of decay, in Vita's words. Sullen and foreign-looking, the snaky flower, scarfed in dull purple, like Egyptian girls, in Virginia's words.

Vita would rather make the children aware of the perfume of flowers which she brings forth through stories of her own invention. Dragging the children away from gorging themselves with red and green gooseberries, she would pull them towards the hedge of sweet-briar and describe the smell that assaults like the great sail of Columbus suddenly catches a strong breeze off the Spice Islands. The clusters of Mimosa which Vita recommends only to be picked when as fluffy and yellow as ducklings, which would lead her to tell the story of the ugly duckling, one of Juliet's favourite. Did Juliet feel Harold's disappointment that his first born grandchild was a girl? She would have felt more acutely the absence of a mother suffering from tuberculosis and incarcerated in hospital or isolated in Philippa's parents' house, than the whims of an ageing grandfather. The Sackville flag was raised for Juliet nonetheless.

The story of mistletoe squatting fruit trees, and which, Vita will again explain, despite some considering it to be a parasite, when treated right, possesses serviceable properties against lightning and thunderbolts, sorcery and witchcraft. Here, Juliet's hand will come to rest in hers. It can extinguish fire: it can discover gold buried in the earth, Vita will go on explaining. "I shall be a fireman", little Adam had once said. Mistletoe can cure ulcers and epilepsy, stimulate fertility in woman and cattle. Juliet will take the golden scissors religiously from Vita's hands – if only gold-plated – never any other metal she advocated for its cutting. Certainly, there is a companionship to be had with this womanhood in the making. The boy has a lovely face to look at, with eyes eating half of it, in ever silent questioning.

But the other granddaughter she sees less often as if the Pepita in her name had altogether estranged her like Vita's own namesake grandmother she never knew; and yet so much a part of her gypsy roots that she ought to love her best. Pepita, so loved by her grandfather that when she died, he had a tiny shoe made in ivory, cut to the shape and size of the sole of one of her dancing shoes.

Harold had again hoped for a boy from Benedict and had privately baptized it Carlo. Was the choice of Pepita an attempt by her son at finding a ground of mutual understanding while he and Vita seem to speak two different languages? It is strange how her own son seems so much of a stranger, while the Florentine Luisa, now separated from Ben, has more common sense. She had by her intelligence and tact been able to improve Ben's attitude towards life, and had brought all that is best in his nature and mind. Moreover, did Luisa not seek her advice on the subject of gardening? However, when Vanessa is in the presence of Nigel's children, she seems so sullen and acts like a spoiled child. Maybe she would act differently if Nigel's wife, Philippa, made her feel more welcome in the family. Vita wishes for her parents to tell Vanessa about their separation instead of keeping the pretence of a united front. Surely, being the daughter of separated parents and of a homosexual father, raised by nannies, does not make life light for a child that young. Did Vita not predict what a funny little mongrel that child would be?

Vita seems to have missed the irony of her thought; or would she have learned her lesson, First Oak wonders, knowing how she had abandoned her boys and left them in the care of nannies in the first years of their life? And was she not herself the daughter of a mongrel mother?

24.

First oak witnessed the death of the Albertines in the severe winter of 1962. They did not cope with Vita's death. She had planted them to the right of the Tower steps, so much a symbol of her blood right to her heritage. The roses blossomed at the same time that Vita found renewed vitality sharing her creative saps with Harold. She chose to depart while the pleasing moments of her garden were at their freshest; before, as Vita put it, the garden loses its look of astonishment at its own youthful candour.

To this day, the canvasses and vistas visitors discover around the gardens and on the walls of Saxingherstes have not faded in the least; as if Vita's hand had just added a penultimate brush stroke, never the last.

The new version of the moyesii, the Rosa Geranium, as delicate as a Chinese drawing, reads like a poem in calligraphy. A lyricism that Vita dispensed throughout the gardens and in her writing.

The Giant Himalayan Lilies still peak their regal heads against the twilight or full moonlight; those sentinels which have so strange a quality of stillness, as Vita said. On many occasions, First Oak has witnessed the lilies stretched out against the silvery silhouette of Vita's revenant presence along the moat.

In the month of Vita's death, the rose garden magnifies its subtle alchemy, mixing its fresh or heady scents; juicy at the humid hours which raise or down the day. Many a visitor, struck by some of the scents, seem to be changed into pillars of salt. It is one of the miracles that Vita wanted to achieve.

And there are other miracles.

Some of the objects made of mutton bones were found in a boot sale; the Saxingherstes' conservationists have recently uncovered the naïve painting made of ink and tears by the French prisoner. It can be admired by the visitors in the Library which used

116

to be Vita and Harold's big room. Vita would have been thrilled by the loop history made to return what rightly belongs to Saxingherste. The painting would have confirmed her intuition was right about the site of the Elizabethan garden within the arms of the moat.

Harold commissioned a skilled letterer to carve a plaque: "Here lived V. Sackville-West who made this garden". How humble the man, how strongly he wanted to make the point that it was first and foremost Vita's garden! Not a far cry from how the yeoman's grave tells of his life: "he tilled the soil well".

Harold's series of strokes tell about his grief after Vita's death, as if a part of himself had died with her. His own death came six years later. His attachment to her compares with the Abutilon Megapotamicum clinging to the sun-soaked wall of which Vita praised the hardiness, the little space it occupies and the fact that it is apt to flower at times when you least expect it, providing an amusing surprise. It needs looking at closely, as if short-sighted, as Vita once said. Had she looked close enough to see how much love Harold had in store for her?

He has had his furious moments too. First Oak had witnessed his outbursts at the visitors as if, with Vita now gone, they were trespassers rather than garden aficionados.

Vita has passed Saxingherstes through to her youngest son, Nigel, in the tradition of the Thomas Sackville's legacy – Knole becoming the junior inheritance - and despite resenting the deprivation of her rights to it. Benedict inherited some of the land and property around Sissinghurst. Likewise, the tradition of being buried in the family vault at Withyham, the birthplace of the family. Following the example of the very first Sackville, and nearly all family members after him, Vita's ashes were placed in the small pink marble urn which had rested on her old desk in the tower.

First Oak knows that it is not only the soil which determines his vital constitution. The sun's energy is necessary to bring water to the top of his branches. Harold and Vita have been those essential energies for each other; one, a nutrients rich soil, the other, the rushing of many waters, sometimes hard or juvenile. Both indispensable.

If only Vita had considered this before she told Harold that she would not have him in Withyham, for the simple reason that he was not of Sackville soil. In Vita's mind however, even a solitary plant ought to flower without encouragement.

Bibliography

The Land
Vita Sackville-West – London William Heinemann Ltd

Vita & Harold – the letters of Vita Sackville-West & Harold Nicolson 1910-1962
edited by Nigel Nicolson

Vita Sackville-West's Sissinghurst – The Creation of a Garden
Vita Sackville-West & Sarah Raven – Virago Press

Sissinghurst An Unfinished History
Adam Nicolson – Viking – Penguin Group

Sissinghurst Castle
Adam Nicolson – National Trust

A House Full of Daughters – extract published in the Sunday Times Magazine
Juliet Nicolson – Chatto & Windus – Penguin Random House

Inheritance – The Story of Knole & The Sackvilles
Robert Sackville-West – Bloomsbury

Behind the Mask – The Life of Vita Sackville-West
Matthew Dennison – William Collins

Have You Been Good? A Memoir
Vanessa Nicolson – Granta Publications

Virginia Woolf
David Daiches – PL Editions Poetry London

Orlando A Biography
Virginia Woolf - Vintage Woolf – Ex Libris